ROMAN ROULETTE

MISSING FRIENDS AND THE MAFIA CAUSE
MAYHEM IN THE MEDITERRANEAN

JANE ELLYSON

A catalogue record for this book is available from the National Library of Australia.

ISBN (paperback): 978-0-6486607-1-2
ISBN (ebook): 978-0-6486607-0-5

Editor: Jackie Bates
Cover Design by nabinkarna on Fiverr
Cover photo of Taormina by Lyle Wilkinson
Italian Map by Scrollavezza on fiverr

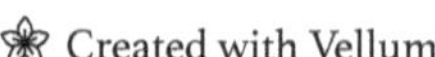 Created with Vellum

CONTENTS

PRAISE FOR ROMAN ROULETTE

Move over James Bond.

∾

Thriller-romance set in Italy. A delayed flight and a missing friend set Charlotte on a whirlwind journey into the world of luxury yachts and nefarious people.

∾

Roman Roulette is a fast-paced thriller set in the world of super models and spies from its opening pages at a party in Rome, to an old vineyard near Taormina.

∾

A young Australian's ingenuity is tested when she accepts an invitation to a party on a yacht.

∾

A delayed journey home and being caught in an unexpectedly menacing place while searching for a friend, reveals capabilities that Charlotte Wyatt never knew she possessed and opportunities that she did not know existed.

ITALIAN MAP

ROME
Italy
NAPLES
MEDITERRANEAN SEA
Tyrrhenian Sea
MESSINA
PALERMO
MOUNT ETNA
TAORMINA
Ionian Sea
Sicily
Mediterranean Sea

PROLOGUE

Charlotte slipped her purchases into her Louis Vuitton carry-on luggage and picked up a copy of the international edition of *The New York Times*. *She was* waiting for her flight to be called for boarding at Rome international airport, and news about the upcoming marriage of Meghan Markle to Harry Windsor was still making front page news. She thought about the prince, Scott, Mason and the elusive Jacques Dessault. Realising she should give Jacques notice about the 'fake news' circulating about his presence at a fashion show in Rome, she dialled his number and was startled when someone immediately answered.

'Yes.'

'May I speak to Jacques please?'

'Who is this?'

'Charlotte Wyatt.'

'And what is your relationship with Jacques?' Charlotte hesitated. What was her relationship with the illusive Frenchman?'

'We're friends.'

'I'm afraid he's tied up at the moment.' The phone rang off. Shaken, Charlotte sat down and absentmindedly flicked through the rest of the paper. On page six there was a small article about a missing industrialist.

The family Dessault has launched a private missing persons investigation and are offering a reward for information related to the whereabouts of Jacques Dessault. The last time he was seen was on the super yacht Taormina Triumph, *in the port of Antibes.*

1

ROME - WEDNESDAY 11 AM

The world stopped. Just for a moment. Charlotte closed the newspaper and glanced nervously around the departure lounge. None of the other passengers were aware of the dangerous notions catapulting around in her head. Where was Jacques and who had answered his phone? He was clearly in trouble. Charlotte's evaluation of alternatives was interrupted by an announcement over the public address system. The first message was in Italian, but she could tell from the tone, it was an apology. Another message followed in English.

'Due to unforeseen circumstances the air traffic controllers are now on an indefinite strike.

Please go to your respective airline counter to rebook your flights and collect your baggage from the carrousel.

We apologise for the inconvenience this has caused to your travel plans.'

Everyone groaned. It was a universal language. Like all the other inconvenienced travellers, she started gathering up her things.

Her phone vibrated. She looked at the caller's ID and smiled.

'Hey Mason.'

'Good. You've not boarded. Guess what?'

'Jacques is officially missing.'

'Ahh. So you've seen the story too. It's a bit concerning don't you think?'

'Even more so because I just called him and someone else answered his phone.'

'Blimey. What did they say?'

'That he was tied up.'

'And ...?'

'That was it. They hung up.'

'Wow. That's –'

'Mason, can I call you back in a couple of hours? It's a bit mad here as there's an air traffic controller strike and I need to get rebooked on a flight tomorrow and get my hotel sorted out for tonight.'

'Righty-oh. Chat later. Ciao.'

There was a long queue at the airline counter. Charlotte was pleased to recognise a few of the girls from yesterday's fashion show. Ayeesha was looking pissed off. Even when she was grumpy, she was magnificent. She was more curvaceous than the other models, with dark brown pouting lips and a gorgeous graze of tiny black curls. She looked like an African Queen and sounded like a radio broadcaster, with a deep voice and generous dollop of dry wit. She'd been keen to get back home to the *real world* in South Africa and escape this *painted party pantomime*, as she described the modelling world. Channing, on the other hand, a Barbie-like beauty from Ukraine, was delighted by the delay and was already on her phone making networking arrangements. She thrived in this world that valued beauty above background and paid generously if you had *the look* to sell highly priced branded goods. Unlike Ayeesha, who had been discovered by chance when a photographer from *Vogue* spotted her in a café in Cape Town, Channing had worked hard to make herself discoverable through postings on Instagram, Facebook and YouTube, and by pitching to every modelling house from New York to Rome. Her new friends greeted her with warm hugs and double kisses. They chatted amiably as they shuffled to the front desk to rebook their tickets and to collect taxi and hotel vouchers. As they pulled their luggage from the trolley at the taxi rank Channing shrieked with delight.

'We're in, girls.'

'We're in what?' Ayeesha replied sceptically.

'Invitation to the hottest party in Rome.'

'Not sure I want to go anywhere where Rome will be burning.'

'We'll be on water so if it gets too fiery for you, you can disembark or jump overboard.'

'Who's hosting the party?' Charlotte asked.

'Sponsors from high end fashion houses along with a Middle Eastern modelling agency. It's being held on a gorgeous yacht. Who knows who you'll rub shoulders with? Lovely food, beautiful people. Opportunities to secure new contracts. You'd be mad not to come.'

'How well do you know these people? Strange things can happen on yachts.' Charlotte spoke with authority.

'Doesn't matter. There'll be tonnes of people you know there and if you feel unsafe, you can simply leave. I'll leave with you. Don't be worried.'

Ayeesha looked at Charlotte and flicked her eyebrows.

'I'll go if you go.'

The *Paradiso* was covered in hundreds of silver and white balloons and thousands of sparkling fairy lights. Eighties music blasted from speakers as the three girls approached the gangplank. Two burly bodyguards, who were twitching a little and clearly not used to wearing ties, regarded the invitation on Channing's phone carefully. They nodded and stepped away from the gangplank.

'Welcome to the party, girls.'

They were immediately greeted by two men with lightly gelled hair, and gym conditioned bodies holding trays of champagne. Channing nodded at the head steward as she walked on deck. Sounds of laughter drew them inside. There was clearly a party mood on board.

Charlotte entered the State Room and had a sense that she'd been here before. It had a different colour scheme and furnishings, but there was something familiar. She kicked up one of the rugs to reveal a beautiful timber floor. Maybe Jacques' yacht had the same flooring? And then she remembered that the room had the same dimensions as the one where she'd first received the bottle from Jacques, back in Antibes. She looked around the room and remembered where they sat and where the camera was. But then she chided herself, reasoning that luxury yachts were probably all the same.

Channing insisted on taking several selfies of the three of them, before Ayeehsa declared enough.

'I'll give this gig thirty minutes then I'm happy to skedaddle. We go together?'

'Sure thing,' her friends replied. Charlotte left Channing and Ayeesha to explore the boat. She met models from countries she'd not heard of, fashion designers, a diplomat from the Australian embassy in France and the Mayor of Rome. There were also representatives from modelling agencies in Italy, Qatar and Saudi Arabia. She participated in dozens of thirty second conversations.

'You're a model?'

'No.'

'A designer?'

'No. I've come with friends who are models. No. I don't know what I am. I do however know what I love. I love beautiful fabrics that sparkle and empower the wearer. I also love travelling, but it makes my parents anxious.'

'I think that's the same for all parents,' one of the agents replied.

'I also don't enjoy being in the spotlight. I'd much rather be in a supporting role than the star on the stage.'

'Then that would be a waste of beauty and intelligence, I'd suspect.' Charlotte was surprised by this unexpected compliment.

'It's Charlotte Wyatt, isn't it?'

Charlotte looked thoughtfully at the woman from the Australian embassy in Paris.

'Yes, it is.'

'You certainly made a colourful splash on the catwalk in Rome,' the woman, who introduced herself as Teal Dubois, commented with a smile. Charlotte wasn't sure if she was making a statement about the makeup or her dramatic departure from the stage.

'Yes, it was an evening few of us will forget,' Charlotte replied, equally ambiguously. 'What brings you to the party?'

'I love fashion, and networking extensively is a part of my job description.' A party for aspiring models did not strike Charlotte as the type of event a government official would attend.

'And what do you do at the embassy?'

'International treaties. Helping to improve trade.'

'That's interesting. And you cover fashion?'

'More textiles and raw goods production like silk, cotton and wool, rather than the modelling industry.' Her reason for being here still didn't make much sense, but Charlotte smiled and accepted the woman's business card and the offer to reach out if she needed anything while she was in Europe.

'Charlotte thanked her before walking down the stairs to explore the lower levels of the super yacht.

The distinctive clicking of a roulette wheel prompted Charlotte to open the first door she came to. The small room hosted a dozen men around a poker table and roulette wheel. A cheer from a man with a distinctly Texan drawl disturbed the relative silence of the room.

'Come join me, sweetheart. My fortunes may have turned with your arrival. Which numbers should I place my winnings on?' Charlotte was surprised by the request, moving closer to the table to view where the others players' chips were located.

'Eight and nine.'

'So be it.' The croupier spun the wheel in one direction and then the ball in the other. The ball bounced around before settling on the six.

'Oh, so close. Let's try again.'

'I don't think I'm a lucky charm.' Charlotte objected.

'You're just warming up. Choose again.'

She hesitated. 'Red thirty-two.' The wheel was spun and the croupier called the end to betting. The ball landed on black twenty-six.

'Sorry,' Charlotte offered.

'You've lost me quite a sum of money young lady. What do you plan to give me as compensation?' His voice had a distinctly menacing undertone. All the men at the table looked at her expectantly.

'I've given you a lesson on the limitations of a lucky charm. Use it wisely.' The men were chuffed at her confident reply and grinned as they lifted their glasses to her in a symbolic touché, confirming she'd hit her mark with her comment. Charlotte left the room quickly, berating herself for having been drawn into their stupid game. She went upstairs and continued her search. Scanning the crowd, she became increasingly anxious until she found Channing. She was deeply engrossed in a conversation with a talent scout.

'Where's Ayeesha?'

'Don't know.'

'I think we should leave. I really think we should leave now,' she added with extra emphasis. Channing turned her head, and stared directly at Charlotte, clearly irritated at having her conversation interrupted.

'One more drink and then we can go. Can you get me a margarita?' she said pointing to the bar. It was a clear signal that she wanted to finish her conversation. Charlotte sighed.

'Of course. One more drink and then we'll go back to the hotel.'

Charlotte threaded her way past several intoxicated girls using the karaoke machine and an enthusiastic juggler.

'What can I get you, lass?' The Irish accent from the bartender with wavy blonde hair and dark rimmed glasses was familiar.

'I'll have a margarita, a soda water with lime and ...' she paused, 'that will be all. No kisses today thank you.'

'Ah so you remember me from The Hop Store in Antibes? *Of all the bars in all the towns in the world, you've walked into mine.* It's a sign.'

'Of what? Bogart would be turning in his grave hearing you strangle his lines like that.'

'Nope. Don't agree. He'd be smiling *back at you kid*.'

'Oh enough, enough. Please get me my drinks so I can get off this floating den of ...' She hesitated to finish the sentence as the barman watched her with curiosity.

'Den of?'

'I don't know. This is not my world. I'm neither a model nor a singer,' she observed wryly, glancing back at the girl on the karaoke machine who had now started belting out a screechy rendition of Helen Reddy's 'I Am Woman'.

'So, what brought you here?'

'I should ask you the same question.'

'It's a bit complicated.'

'For me too.' They both laughed

'Two Heinekens please,' came a surly request from a man in a crinkled, silver suit with a black shirt and leery demeanour.

'Of course, sir. Right up.'

Charlotte checked her phone while the barman with a name badge *Roy* on his crisp shirt, pulled the beers. No messages. She tried to call Ayeesha and went straight through to voicemail. Time to venture below once more to see if she could find her. She passed the gambling room, a storage room, a crew bunk room and was headed to a door near the end of the passage when a uniformed crew member with a stubbly chin suddenly appeared and stopped her.

'Those are the captain's quarters. Out of bounds for visitors unless you've received a *personal* invitation.'

'My apologies. I didn't mean to trespass. I was looking for the bathroom.'

'Down the end on your right.'

'Thank you.' Charlotte walked to the door he had pointed at and gave him a wave as she entered, locking the door behind her. She leant over the basin to wash her face. As she patted her face dry, she examined the walls of the small room. A small safety notice caught her attention. It was for *The Taormina Triumph*. Charlotte instantly knew that this was the yacht that Jacques had been working on when she last saw him on March 22 in Antibes. This did not feel right. Why had the name of the yacht changed? Had the boat been sold or stolen? As her mind raced through what she knew as fact and what were assumptions, she became aware that she could hear the gentle humming of the yacht's engines. The boat was leaving. She was in danger and needed to get herself and her friends off the yacht, fast. She ran up the stairs and was distraught to see the lights of the city twinkling in the distance. She was a captive, at least until the next port of call.

'Who's this?'

Charlotte carefully regarded the man with the thick reddish eyebrows, joined uncomfortably as one. His piercing green eyes unnerved her, and that thin red stubbly chin was unmistakable. This was the man she'd encountered outside the captain's cabin earlier that evening.

'An accidental stowaway, Rex. She was in the casino when we cast off. Didn't hear the announcement,' Roy said.

'I see. No problem. She can come all the way to Taormina and work with the other models,' Rex replied.

'I'm not a model. I mean, I no longer wish to be a model,' Charlotte spluttered.

'There's a lot of money for just for a few hours of your time,' Rex said

'Thanks again. I have to get home. My parents are waiting for me. They'll call out the national guard if I'm not home soon.'

'You told them you were coming on the *Paradiso*?' Rex said. Charlotte thought this question strange and was immediately on guard.

'Well yes, of course and I've already sent them *loads* of pictures from the party.'

'I see. Yes. It's best you get off in Naples and go home to your parents.'

Charlotte was lying, of course. She hadn't been the slightest bit interested in taking photos on the yacht. And she hadn't been in contact with her parents since the airport. There was something *off* about Rex.

'I think you should make yourself useful.'

'What?' Charlotte replied, now wary of everything he said.

'There's dishes to wash and floors to mop.'

'Happy to help,' Charlotte responded with a smile.

Unsure of how to read this perky Australian Cinderella, he shook his head and shuffled off to the bridge.

Charlotte peppered Roy with questions as he led her to the store room where he gave her crisp white shorts and a monogrammed crew polo shirt to change into. She was pleased to learn that Channing had literally *run off* the ship, but was annoyed that she hadn't thought to look for her before she did. Now, more comfortable in crew clothing, she joined Roy in the galley unpacking glasses from the dishwasher.

At just after 2:00am they made their way down to the crew dormitory. Charlotte was again struck by a sense of déjà vu.

'This was the bunk I had last time,' she muttered as she sniffed the bed covers.

'To your liking my lady?' Roy asked quizzically.

'Oops, sorry. This is perfect. Just like home.' She climbed onto the bunk. 'Roy?'

'Yes?'

'Who owns this yacht?'

'A consortium of owners. And no, before you ask, I don't know any of them, although I'm pretty sure Rex is related to one of them.'

'Why?'

'Because he certainly didn't get the job for his interpersonal skills.'

'You don't need good interpersonal skills to be an engineer,' she replied.

'On a yacht, even one this large, getting along with all

sorts of other people is key because we're in such close proximity.'

'I see.' Changing tack, Charlotte asked Roy a more personal question.

'So why did you leave the bar in Antibes?"

'It was only ever a casual role. Not a profession. I like sailing but in my other life, I'm a Data Architect. I'm currently on sabbatical, travelling towards the Greek Islands, picking up work along the way and like you, I'm also looking for someone.'

'Are you? Who?'

'My sister, Niamh. She'd be younger than you but equally independently minded. She went to Corsica on a sailing holiday with a friend. My parents got an excited message saying that she'd met a fella and wasn't coming back. This message wasn't so surprising, but when they tried to call her, the phone went to voice mail and they then received a bizarre message telling them to stop trying to contact her. Alarm bells went off as she'd never send a message like that. Something was amiss.'

'Mum and Dad would've gone ballistic,' Charlotte said.

'Yeah. Mine were nervous. They contacted the police who made a few enquiries but said that it didn't qualify as a missing person case yet. She was of age and had clearly shacked up with some bloke she'd met. They were sure she'd come home in her own good time. My parents then called me. My task is to find someone who doesn't want to be found. Here's her photo. Don't suppose you've seen her?'

Charlotte looked at the photo of the elf-like girl; alabaster skin, wide eyes, straight, shoulder-length, straw-berry-coloured hair and a mischievous grin.

'She's lovely, but no, I've not seen her. Sorry.' Charlotte

snuggled under the covers. Roy reached out and turned off the light.

'Goodnight Charlotte.'

'Night Roy.'

As Charlotte let the gentle movement of the yacht lull her to sleep, she thought about Ayeesha. She must have got off the boat after all, just like Channing had. She certainly hoped so, but not answering her phone, well, that was just not like her.

A few hours later she was woken by a familiar juddering sound. A helicopter was landing on the yacht. She slipped out of her bunk and crept up the stairs. Someone had just stepped away from the helicopter to speak with a crew member. There was something about the way he held his body and turned his head which were familiar. Fear enveloped her as she recognised The Monk talking with Rex, metres away from the rotating blades. The two men hugged, and her erstwhile kidnapper returned to the helicopter, before it lifted off and quickly disappeared into the darkness. Charlotte slipped back down the stairs to the bunk house. She had good reason to be afraid for Ayeesha, and indeed for herself.

2

CHANNING'S STORY

All her life Channing had wanted to be famous. Movie star posters adorned her bedroom wall. And the dream of escaping from dreary Ukraine, kept her sustained through the dark period of her parents' messy divorce. She was not the prettiest girl in class. But she was the most determined. With natural height and a reasonable bone structure, she worked hard at keeping fit and eating well. Eventually she earnt enough money to have plastic surgery, tweaking her body to fit the requirements of the fashion magazines.

Most days were spent sending out her portfolio to modelling agencies. One had answered with an invitation to come to Rome to appear in an oriental catwalk at the St Regis Hotel. She'd already made useful contacts and was keen to seize every opportunity. Anything she could do to avoid getting on the plane and going back to live with her mother in Kiev in their tiny apartment.

At the party, the clearly gay talent scout had been enthusiastic about her potential. He assured her it would be easy to gain future modeling work if she attended the private party and catwalk near Taormina in Sicily. He'd asked her lots of questions about her aspirations and her family situation. She'd thanked him profusely, rushing off the yacht to get a taxi back to the hotel to collect her things. She didn't for a moment think to tell Charlotte she was going, assuming she'd be back before Charlotte had even noticed that she was gone. The traffic, however, was heavier than expected. And with a heavy heart, she arrived at the port to see the *Paradiso* sailing off into the sunset.

Channing was determined. She immediately caught a taxi to Naples, knowing that this single event would wipe out her credit card limit. It was what you needed to do in pursuit of your professional goals. She was delighted to see the super yacht coming into dock as the taxi dropped her at the port.

3

NAPLES - THURSDAY MORNING

Flickering lights and the sound of fog horns broke the stillness of the morning as they pulled into the port of Naples. Charlotte's phone suddenly had a signal. There was a message from her parents.

Disappointing news about the strike. Keep safe and keep in touch.

She replied:

She'd googled transport options available for a return to Rome and decided to take the train. There was someone frantically waving at her from the dock as they pulled into port. Charlotte groaned. It was Channing.

'Hey Charlotte. You look a bit tired? Partying all night? Give me a wave so I can snap you for my socials.' Channing shouted through cupped hands so she could be heard above the engine noise.

'No thanks, Channing,' she said with a wave, putting a hand in front of her face as the yacht inched towards the jetty. The yacht docked and Charlotte ran down the gangplank, blocking Channing's entry on board.

'Come with me. Let's go get coffee and you can tell me all about the people you met last night.'

'Why don't we chat on board? I'd hate to get left behind again.'

'Because I need to buy clothes. Mine are still back at the hotel and I need your expert guidance. The yacht won't depart till after lunch. We've plenty of time' This was a lie.

Channing looked at Charlotte's white crew uniform and nodded.

'Understand. Of course. But I don't want to carry my bag around shopping. Let me leave it on board and say Hi.'

'No time,' Charlotte replied quickly. 'Give it to me and I'll pop it on the deck.' Before she could respond, Charlotte had grabbed her bag and thrown it on the upper deck. She ran back down the gangplank and looped her arm through Channing's.

'Come. Shopping awaits.'

All Charlotte needed was an hour. Roy had said that they wanted a quick turnaround in Naples as there were keen to get to Taormina. If she could just keep Channing sufficiently distracted and away from the port, the yacht would leave without them. Charlotte asked her if she'd seen Ayeesha at the hotel. She shook her head. Nor had she made enquiries when she was collecting her things. She was completely unconcerned by Ayeesha's disappearance and suggested she'd met a nice man, and not wanted to be discovered. Perhaps Channing was right, and she was overthinking things.

Charlotte had purchased a handful of essential clothes and toiletries and Channing was pressuring her to return to the yacht. She looked at her phone. Ninety minutes had passed and with a slow walk back to the port, she was certain the *Paradiso* would have departed. But Channing was having none of it.

'Hurry up. Don't wanna get left behind.' She scurried ahead, not waiting for Charlotte, and literally ran into Scott Harmon, who was coming out of a yachting supplies store. The clink of metal cups bouncing on cobbled stones drew the attention of other shoppers. Charlotte bent down to scoop them up.

'Charlotte? Why aren't you on your way back to Brisbane?'

'Air traffic control strike.'

'Umm. But why are you here in Naples?'

'We're on our way to Taormina to a fashion show, and we're running late,' Channing snapped, grabbing Charlotte by the hand, and pulling her down the street.'

'Oh, it's gone,' Channing shouted at Charlotte in annoyance. 'It's all your fault. You and your damn clothes. A loud whistle rang out from their left.

'Over here ladies. We're waiting for you.' The *Paradiso* had moved locations and Channing was now in full flight, awkwardly running towards it in her high heels. Charlotte's subterfuge had failed. She couldn't stop Channing getting on the boat and was afraid for her. She hesitated momentarily and looked back to Scott who had not yet caught up with them.

'Gotta go,' she said to him and ran along the dockside to the yacht and up the gang plank. Rex, the man who looked eerily like Van Gogh, addressed her with a smirk.

'Changed your mind I see. Welcome back.'

Creepy Rex was standing beside her on the upper deck when Scott called her mobile. She managed a few crisp and factual replies before the signal was lost. She would have liked to have outlined her fears about Ayeesha, but didn't want to do so within earshot of this man who'd been hugging her tormentor the previous evening. Keeping close to Channing so she was safe, was now a higher priority.

'This is more my style,' Channing cooed as they were shown to a guest cabin with large twin beds. Charlotte noted the impact of elevation from crew to guest status immediately as she sat on the firm mattress, the bed adorned by half a dozen pillows replete with gold and silver tassels. They'd not need the bed, though, as they'd be arriving into Taormina early evening and would be taken to 'The Vineyard' which was the site of the gala event.

There was an itinerary on the bedside table, although the word *itinerary*, was generous.

> *Arrive Vineyard.*
> *Place personal items in lockers.*
> *Meet on terrace for briefing.*
> *Explanation of rules.*
> *Fashion show and mingling.*

There were four other models on board who had been picked up in Naples. They were as excited as Channing by the opportunities promised by the gala event. They were all early in their careers and had been invited to this event, after being unsuccessful in their attempts to be selected for the Summer Festival Fashion parade in Naples. They considered this a most wonderful consolation prize. A return ticket to Taormina from Naples was an invitation too good to refuse, particularly when there was only six hours of 'work' involved.

They were offered cocktails and canapés on the upper deck. Charlotte was surprised that Roy wasn't serving them.

'Where's Roy?' she asked while taking the flute of champagne from the silver tray.

'He got off in Naples,' the waiter responded. That's odd, she thought. One of the models leaned over and whispered in her ear.

'Got into a bit of a scuffle with the *Overlord* who didn't take too kindly to Roy asking the girls if they'd seen his sister. Long shot if you ask me, asking us. The world is a big place to disappear into.'

'Ahh. thank you ...?'

'Stella. Stella from Slough, near Heathrow.' Charlotte wasn't sure why this additional geographic precision was needed.

'Thanks Stella.'

'I'm on my own escape path. No way my parents would let me come all the way to Sicily on my own. Don't approve of my ambitions to be a model. Think it'll make me anxious, well, more anxious. This trip will give me a chance to prove them wrong.'

'I hope you're right, Stella,' Charlotte replied with conviction.

So many people were missing. Roy was looking for his sister Niamh. Ayeesha had disappeared without saying goodbye and Jacques Dessault's family had officially declared him missing.

Channing slumped down beside Charlotte on a long bench seat.

'Tell me about that guy we bumped into on the port. Who's he? He's cute.'

'Scott Harmon. He's my best friend Miranda's brother.'

'Do you know him very well?' Charlotte bit her lip as she considered the question. She remembered the wonderful day they'd spent touring the Côte d'Azur with Mason Murray, who was a journalist for *Hello* magazine and Scott's best friend. More recently, she'd been riding on the back of a Vespa with Scott as they toured Rome. She remembered the delicious taste of the stracciatella gelato as they looked out over the city from Palatine Hill and the softness of his lips as he said goodbye.

'Quite well. We were members of the same surfing club in Byron Bay.'

'Is he seeing anyone?'

'I honestly don't know.'

'Unlikely that someone that good-looking is available. Still, we can but hope.'

4

ROY REFLECTS - ONE HOUR EARLIER

He was psychotic. Raging Rex was definitely psychotic. How was showing people a photo of my sister a problem? What to do now? Find another job or go home? Nope. I've got to keep looking. Someone, somewhere must have seen Niamh. I'll consider the options over breakfast.

Roy scribbled down the names of the places he'd already visited on the back of a beer mat as he leaned against the bar. He'd started in Corsica, then caught a ferry across to Nice, visiting Monaco, Antibes and Cannes. He'd then caught a train to Genoa in Italy where he'd met a purser in a yachting supplies store who'd offered him the barman role on the *Paradiso*. The yacht had visited Livorno and Rome before he was unceremoniously dumped in Naples. He'd hoped to visit the major ports in Sicily before heading east to Greece. He could still do this.

He glanced around the busy café, looking at at the clientele. Well-heeled women sipped their cappuccinos and chatted amiably across tiny tables. Hurried businesspeople downed their espressos in two gulps before calling *Grazie!*

on their way out. There were crew members discussing last minute purchasing requirements. He scanned this group to identify a friendly face he could pitch to. There was a first officer on his own ordering at the end of the bar. Scott looked his way and Roy caught his eye.

5

SCOTT DELIBERATES

What the hell was Charlie Girl going to do in Taormina? Scott pondered, as he watched the yacht head out into the open water. Had she made plans to get back to Rome from Sicily? She'd find that a challenge with no planes due to the strike. Damn she was infuriating, risk-taking, bloody-minded, and so, so... lovely. He remembered how starstruck he'd been by her presence on the catwalk in Rome; how afraid he was when he knew The Monk was only metres away from her; and how relieved he was when he'd scooped her up in his arms and carried her away to safety. He also remembered kissing her in her hotel room. The gorgeous scent of her. The softness of her skin. He'd had to leave, not only because he had provisions to collect, but because he'd wanted to stay. To get to know her better, to... Scott shook his head unconsciously, forcing a change in focus. He knew her parents and particularly her mother wouldn't want her to go unaccompanied to Sicily, a country with a reputation for mobsters. Having lost one child, they were particularly anxious for her safety and had tried to keep her from travelling to the other side of the world.

Whose boat was she on now? If he wanted to ask her, he'd need to do so before she sailed out of signal range. He picked up his phone.

'Yes,' Charlotte responded cautiously to his call.

'It's Scott.'

'I know.'

'Um. What are you doing?'

'I'm going to a modelling event near Taormina. At a vineyard. Should be fun,' she said nervously.

'I thought you'd given up modelling.'

'So did I.' This response confused Scott.

'And how are you getting back to Rome?'

'All arranged. Return tickets are part of the package for participating.'

'Who's organising this event?'

'Yes, I agree it's too cold for swimming.' And then the signal cut.

Why did she talk about swimming? Why didn't she say who'd organised the damn event? Scott looked at his watch and realised he only had forty minutes before the yacht he was working on was due to depart for Palermo via Messina. He'd grab a coffee and try to figure out how to convince her to get back to Rome as soon as possible.

The café was small and crowded. He liked the way Italians stood at the bar and tipped their espresso dramatically down their throats. He ordered a coffee and leaned on a bar stool. Someone at the other end of the bar was looking at him. The tall man wearing slightly dishevelled crew clothing, moved towards him and put his hand out.

'I'm Roy. Wondering if you needed a barman or deckhand on your vessel.'

'We've met before I think. Where do I know you from, Roy?' he asked as they shook hands.

'In France. I was working in the Hop Store in Antibes when you were having a drink with friends last month.'

'Yes, I remember you now. You rascal. You were enforcing the *no kissing* rule.' Roy grinned and Scott stroked his chin as a smile crept across his face. 'I'm very time poor but you've got sixty seconds. What's your story?'

'Been a kitchen hand, deckhand and barman. Most recently worked on the *Paradiso*. I'm reliable, hardworking, team player, funny, good with the ladies and ...'

'Humble?' Scott prompted.

'But of course. I'm from Belfast.'

'Well as Irish luck would have it, we could use an extra pair of hands. The yacht is moored third from the end. Pushing off in thirty minutes.'.

'Ready to go.' Roy announced as he slung his bag over his shoulder.

'Quanto?' Scott signalled for the bill with his hand to the barman.

Scott paid their bill and they exited together.

'Did I hear you say you'd been on the *Paradiso*?'

'Yep.'

'That just left?'

'Uh-huh.'

'Why aren't you on it now?'

'Difference of opinion with the chief engineer.'

'About what?'

'He didn't like me asking staff if they'd seen my sister.'

'Why, was she crew?'

'She may have been. She's a good sailor. But to be honest I'm clutching at straws. I'm asking anyone I meet, if they've seen her. I asked your friend Charlotte as well. She was a guest on the yacht and also looking for someone.'

'Who?'

'Another model. Ayeesha I think her name was. Don't know her. She left the party on the *Paradiso* in Rome without saying goodbye and Charlotte thinks that means that ...' he hesitated, 'something nefarious has happened to her. I understand her concerns because my sister's missing too.'

Scott shook his head, hit the screen on his phone and started texting.

Keep your strava app on Charlie Girl!'

6

———

TAORMINA, THURSDAY EVENING

The snowy peak of Mount Etna was visible through the clouds as they sailed towards Giardini Naxos, the small port closest to Taormina. The smoking mountain looked majestic and added to the excitement of the trip.

'Do we get time for sightseeing?' one of the girls asked.

'Yes of course. Plenty of time tomorrow,' the purser replied. She beamed at him, delighted. Charlotte's brow furrowed. The man's smile looked convenient.

Charlotte glanced at Scott's text, which appeared as they moved closer to shore. She smiled and did as instructed after sending back a startled emoji. She hoped he'd picked up the signal that all was not well from her swimming comment. She could already hear him saying *I told you so*, next time they caught up.

The enchanting town was comfortably snuggled into rocky cliffs. The girls were transported ashore by smaller watercraft. Charlotte briefly considered making her own escape as her feet touched solid ground. It would be easy. She could simply refuse to get in the waiting minivan, make a huge fuss and they'd be pleased to get rid of her. But she'd come to keep Channing safe, and now she felt an obligation to protect Stella and the other models as well.

The girls chatted excitedly as the minivan wove its way up the hills and into the countryside. Forty minutes later, having travelled past a solid wrought-iron gate with a large field behind it, which could easily have served as a dealership for Italian sports cars, they arrived. Music was wafting down the hill from a large stone country house and the sun was slowly setting, creating orangey hues atop the vineyard.

'Anyone else lost their internet signal?' Channing asked. She'd been scrolling through Instagram photos for the previous twenty minutes. Universal nods from the other girls confirmed that they were indeed in the wilderness.

'This is a huge problem for me,' she said, exasperated.

They drove up the hill past rows of vines on a potholed road, not suitable for most vehicles. Charlotte ran over the number of turns they had taken since leaving the outskirts of Taormina in her head. Just in case. As the minivan pulled to a stop, the large arched doors of the country house opened and a man in a bespoke suit stepped out.

'Welcome, ladies.'

Charlotte shivered. It was The Monk. She instinctively reached into her bag for the sun hat and dark glasses that had been purchased hastily in Naples. A disguise was needed.

She was the last to dismount from the bus and did so with an exaggerated stagger. The Monk leaned forward to take her arm and reached to remove her sunglasses.

'Nein,' she screeched. 'Zu viel zu trinken. I've had too much to drink on the boat.' Startled, he withdrew his hand.

'Badezimmer. I need the bathroom,' she cried as she put her hand over her face.

'Down the hall on your left. Be quick. We're running late. The briefing is starting now on the back terrace.' Charlotte nodded and ran inside as though she was about to vomit. She passed the bathroom on the ground floor and tiptoed up the staircase. At the top of the stairs, she turned left, listening carefully for voices or footsteps. No one had followed her. She tried the door handles of several rooms. All locked. The third one along was open, so she quietly entered and shut the door behind her. She removed her hat, glasses and sundress and put her crew clothes back on. They would provide temporary cover while she looked for a way to get Channing and Stella away from this place. She looked out the window, staring in awe at the circus-like set up on the other side of the house, far away from the eyes of passing traffic. There were several large marquees positioned at opposite ends of the vineyard and a row of connected tents in the middle which was presumably where the catwalk was set up. On the horizon, beyond two gently rolling hills of symmetrical vines, Charlotte could see the sea. A familiar voice screeching '*No!*' caught her attention and she moved closer to the window to see Channing resisting a request to surrender her mobile phone to one of the concierges. Laughter from the room next door could be heard, which was clearly in response to the scene playing out on the terrace. She put her ear to the wall and listened. Two men were chatting in Italian. She didn't understand what they were saying and regretted not having taken lessons in Italian at school as she had for French and German.

Her eyes scanned the room. A silver tray on a sideboard and small fridge in the corner gave her an idea. She tidied her hair into a bun, and arranged several beers from the fridge on the tray. She knocked on the door to the room where the men were laughing and called out '*Drinks.*'

'Sì.'

Charlotte walked confidently towards the men sitting at a large table with several computers, security screens and black boxes. There were two phones on the table with full signal functionality. They took the drinks from the tray and one of the men snapped at her.

'Why have you not changed? Go. Now. Along the corridor. Pronto. The show starts shortly. All waiting staff are wearing black and white.' Charlotte hesitated and the quieter of the two men, rose from his chair, signalled for her to follow and walked her down the corridor to a small room, where an elderly lady was ironing shirts.

'Ancora uno. One more uniform,' he said pointing at the clothing hanging on the ironing rack. He left before she had a chance to respond.

The woman moved to the rack and pulled off a pair of black trousers, a crisp white cotton shirt and maroon vest with gold embroidery, not unlike the cushions on the yacht. The words *Vittoria d'oro Vineyard* appeared beneath a coat of arms on the collar of the shirt.

Charlotte took the clothes back to the room beside the one with the security cameras, and closed the door gently. She looked at her phone. No signal, which was surprising as she could hear the men next door answering their own phones. They must somehow be blocking the major signal providers, with their own phones connected to another network. Charlotte considered what would be required to stop the jamming signal, if only for a short moment, so she could call the police. But what would she say? And how long would it take for them to get here? They were miles from a major town. She didn't need to work through the detail of this plan as a simpler opportunity suddenly arose. One of the other men was called downstairs, and the remaining technician left for the bathroom. Charlotte moved quickly into the control room and scooped up the mobile phone that had been left behind. She glanced at the video screens and could see that there were cameras everywhere. The sound of a toilet flushing sent Charlotte rushing down the stairs, carefully slipping the phone into her trouser pocket. Remembering the cameras, she embraced her role as server, and warmly greeted guests, asking them if they needed drinks as she made her way to the bar at the end of the terrace.

'Who are you?' the barman asked accusingly.' I've not seen you before.'

'I'm new. Rex recruited me in Naples after an incident with one of the team. Roy was *asked* to leave,' she responded with due emphasis. The man regarded her sceptically.

'Very well. You are assigned to the two tents, on the right, only. Capisci?' Charlotte nodded, guessing that he was asking her if she understood. 'For the band,' he announced placing six beers on the tray in front of her. She carefully balanced the drinks and headed down the hill to the tent where she could hear the sounds of a band sound-checking.

There was a security guard at the entrance who opened the flap for her as she arrived. The drinks were gratefully received, and she was surprised to see a Grammy Award-winning singer giving instructions to the lighting technicians. Breezy was an international singing sensation. Her trademark blonde mohawk had colourful splashes of pink and blue. Charlotte assumed that she must be receiving a hefty commission for singing for guests at this relatively small event. As she left the tent a whistle demanded her attention from the next marquee.

'We need you over here.'

Charlotte scurried over and slipped inside the second marquee. 'This table, and that one over there, need drinks.' She was astounded to see three members of the Italian Carabinieri at the first poker table. There would be no need to call the police as they were already here. She could not be sure who, or what, they were here to protect. The whirring of the roulette wheel immediately transported her back to the gambling room below deck on the *Paradiso*.

It was a mini-United Nations inside this Arabian Nights themed den, with well-dressed gamblers seated around tables speaking Russian, French, English, Italian and Arabic. They paid her scant attention as she took their orders and delivered their drink requests. This was however not the case at the far roulette table, where a tall African man dressed in noble robes, stared at her.

'Surely, madam, you should be in the next tent, on the catwalk. You are indeed a rare beauty.'

'You flatter me sir and your kind words are appreciated.'

'Ahhh. She possesses tact as well as wonderful features.' He shaped an hourglass with his hands. The men around the table leered at Charlotte in the measured way one would assess a racehorse. An elderly man with skin covered in pock marks reached out to pat her bottom and she quickly pirouetted away from the table and curtseyed. Another man asked her to light his cigar for her. He held his gold lighter in his hand, forcing her to move back to the table to take it and he leaned towards her expectantly. He reeked of garlic and a lack of attention to dental hygiene. She lit the cigar, while he stared at her with intimidating eyes and then passed the lighter back to him.

'Keep it, my darling. My number is engraved on it, for your convenience.' He wrapped his hand around hers so that she held the lighter in the palm of her hand.

'Again, thank you and enjoy your evening.' Charlotte slipped the lighter into her pocket, nodded at the head waiter and promptly left the tent. Emerging into the darkness, she could hear the band playing in the marquee to her left and polite clapping from inside the marquee to her right. The opening address must have finished. Remembering the security cameras, she readjusted her posture and walked purposefully up the hill, smiling at patrons on their way down to the music and gambling marquees. As she approached the main terrace, she raised her hand as though she had been called and headed towards the models' changing room tent. She was relieved to see Channing, immaculately decked out as an ancient Egyptian queen. Her blonde hair was hidden under a black bob wig, with tiny chains circling the crown of her head. A strapless, figure-hugging dress of turquoise was accompanied by a magnificent gold and emerald piece sitting high around her neck.

'Wow.'

'Where've you been, Charlotte? What are you wearing? And there's a man looking for you.'

'Youngish. Italian. Dark curly hair?'

'No. Fair haired. Early forties. Could be Swiss, Italian or French. He was asking for the *German model* who I guess is you as we are a model short. I didn't know you were German?'

'I'm not.'

'I don't understand.'

'I know. You've gotta trust me Channing. Things are not

as they seem. For one, I'm sure they're jamming the network so there's little communication out of here. However, I managed to pick up a phone which has a signal.'

'By picked up, you mean?'

'Borrowed it. OK. I stole it and there's probably an angry Italian turning everything upside down as he looks for it, or me.'

'You thief. I had no idea.'

'Look Channing, this is serious. Can you send a message out on Instagram that Breezy's playing at Vittoria d'oro Vineyard?'

'Serious. You're pulling my leg?'

'No. I'm not. She's here – warming up in the marquee at the end.'

'I wonder if they'll let us go and watch later.'

'I think they have other, far less pleasant things in store for you.'

'What do you mean?'

'I don't know yet. But I do know that there are some truly bad people here. I need to get you and the other models out. And the easiest way to do this is to get lots of people here. Send the message, hide the phone and keep your wits about you.'

'Channing, you're next,' Stella announced. 'Charlotte? Where've you been?'

'Shhh,' Charlotte whispered, her finger pressed to her lips, as she slipped out under the back flap of the tent.

There was heavy security at the opening to the largest marquee where the fashion parade was taking place. Invitations were rigorously scrutinised before each guest was permitted entry. Upon approval they were given a small black device the size of a pack of cards. No serving staff were entering or leaving, and she remembered the specific instructions that she was only to serve guests in the gambling and music marquees. Charlotte walked carefully around the back of the tent and examined the canvas for any peep holes. There were none. There was however a flap in the far corner that had not been securely tied so she lay down on the damp grass, lifted the flap and peered inside.

The catwalk was decorated in an east-Asian style, not dissimilar to the one she had walked on in Rome, with bold multi-coloured taffetas framing the stage and runway and huge chandeliers hanging from the highest point in the centre of each tent. The Roman event was clearly where the Monk has sourced his idea, and indeed there he was, sitting front and centre, in the middle of his extravaganza.

Above the stage was an electronic board. As each model strutted up the runway, guests used their devices to score them. Charlotte disliked this objectifying of the women and wondered what purpose it served. Channing appeared on the runway and was clearly enjoying her moment in the spotlight. She smiled and sauntered as the audience murmured their appreciation. Many of the men in the audience, and they were all men, were dressed in dark blue or grey suits. They had the look, typically seen in the board member section of a company's annual report. The scoreboard lit up and there was a fracas between two guests when one of the devices appeared to fail. The Monk settled the guests with a reassuring wave and clicked his fingers, pointing to the scoreboard. The scoreboard was reset to zero and the rating process recommenced. But it wasn't a rating process. It was a bidding war with each of the models for sale. And Channing was oblivious to it all. She exited the stage with a regal wave.

Charlotte stood, wondering what the Monk's process was for getting the models to *quietly leave* with their acquirers. This would be an impossible process for spirited Channing, indeed for all of them. And how were they going to get them out of the country? As she pondered what logistically would be needed, she became aware that her uniform was soiled and covered in grass. One problem at a time. She set off to explore the boundaries and possible escape routes from this sordid marketplace.

Charlotte was grateful for the bright moon revealing a narrow path between two rows of vineyards heading down to the sea. This was the only other obvious exit from the property. As an escape route, the main road was bound to be full of the Monk's men and it would be impossible to know who to trust. She wasn't sure what lay at the end of the path, but felt confident that she could find her way back to Taormina by following the coastline. The sound of approaching footsteps forced her further down the path and she hid behind a mature olive tree. She recognised the man from the security room. He unzipped his trousers and urinated on the path. *Men,* Charlotte cursed under her breath. He lit a cigarette, took a long drag, and watched the smoke float away. His phone rang breaking his reverie. The person calling was not Italian so there was a disjointed conversation in English and French. Charlotte understood the following from the call:

- *He reported that he was checking the perimeter.*
- *He was told to immediately go to the front gate as*

people, including reporters, were wanting to speak with the rock star Breezy.

- *Confirmed the girls were secure and delivery could start when directed.*
- *And no, Marco had not yet found his phone. A joke followed about it having been accidentally dropped down the toilet.*

He rang off and threw his cigarette on the ground, further annoying Charlotte. Given that he'd lied about checking the perimeter, it was possible he needed to check that the girls were secure. Charlotte kept one hundred metres behind him as he walked through the vineyard in the shadows of the music marquee, gambling marquee and runway marquee. On the far side of the clearing was another tent, this one the size of a small bedroom. It was positioned in front of a crumbling stone cottage which had lost its fight with the wild olive trees. Something shiny reflected against the house lights and Charlotte crept behind the cottage to discover two helicopters not far away, resting on concrete platforms. There was a small hole in the damaged wall at the back of the cottage and Charlotte peered in. She couldn't see anything but could hear movement. Taking a calculated risk, she flicked the cigarette lighter on and was taken aback at the sight of four girls, bound and gagged. They started murmuring and hitting their feet against the floor, attracting the attention of the person in the tent in front of the cottage who pushed the old timber door open and punched the nearest offender, prompting the others to settle. Charlotte ran back in the direction of the main tents and was horrified to see Channing strolling up to the tent in front of the cottage.

'Channing. No. Where are you going?'

'To get paid. I was apparently a big hit and will be receiving a bonus. That's the payment tent. What happened to you? 'she said, looking at Charlotte's stained uniform.

'No time to tell. But there's no one at the tent now. I've just come from there. Do you still have that phone?'

'Yes.'

'Then why don't you talk your way into the music marquee and share *The Breezy Experience* with all your followers.'

'Great idea. Ta. Thanks for thinking of me.'

'More than you know. Now go.'

Charlotte skipped around the back of the tents again and returned to the main bar. The barman looked aghast.

'One of our guests wanted to get to know me better,' she offered by way of explanation. 'I need to change my uniform. I'll be back in a moment.'

The barman was relieved that she wasn't making a fuss and waved his hand, giving her permission to change. She scooted up the stairs and into the uniform room. The woman who had been ironing on her last visit was no longer there. She took a black uniform, like the one the security guards were wearing, from the rack knowing it would be harder to be seen at night. A pair of scissors were on a table near the ironing board. Pausing only for a moment, she quickly cut off her shoulder length hair and hung the scissors from her belt. As she checked the pockets of her soiled uniform, she found the gold cigarette lighter and an idea formed. She had to wait for Channing's Instagram followers to arrive and she didn't have to wait long. The shouting through the security system sent the remaining guard rushing down the stairs in the direction of the front gate. She sprayed a bottle of methylated spirits she'd found in the ironing room on anything that looked flammable. While she was scrunching paper into the waste paper bin her eyes scanned the cameras. Some of the guests were leaving the gambling tent to investigate the shouts coming from the main road.

Channing had been thrown out of the music marquee and was arguing with the doorman. Charlotte started pulling all the plugs out of the machines, hoping that one of these actions would open up the mobile networks. She lit a fire in the bin and grabbed the closest black box and threw it out the window, onto the roof of the terrace. The sound of splintering glass echoed across the valley. A woman screamed as the box bounced off the roof and onto the lawn. The fire climbed up the walls and Charlotte dropped the lighter and shouted, 'Fire! Fire!' before climbing through the window onto the terrace tiles, and shimmying down a drain-pipe. People were panicking and starting to run for their cars. Chaos reigned.

Charlotte ran directly to the tent in front of the small cottage and demanded that the guard help with the fire. He was confused. He didn't know this thin young man in the black uniform but was used to following directions, particularly from people with obvious authority. He ran towards the house while Charlotte threw her weight against the cottage door several times without success. She ran around the back of the cottage and began pulling at the small stones of the damaged wall until a passage was cleared. The girls awkwardly crawled out through the hole and Charlotte cut their gags and bindings before leading them behind the marquees down to the coastal path. The distinct sound of a fire engine's siren could be heard in the distance. As she reached *urination point* at the top of the vineyard, she could hear Channing screaming. She looked at the girls, and then at Channing who was outside the entrance to the music tent. Pointing down the path, Charlotte whispered '*Run!*' They took off like startled rabbits and were out of sight in seconds.

Channing was now being carried like a sack of potatoes towards the helicopters. Grabbing an olive tree branch, Charlotte ran at full force towards the guard. The branch went hard against the back of his knees and he screamed, fell to the ground, and dropped his load. Channing scrambled to her feet and looked at Charlotte bewildered, still not appreciating the imminent danger she was in.

'Go. Firemen are here. Run.' Charlotte screamed. Channing kicked off her shoes and sprinted up the hill with the guard in pursuit. Charlotte pivoted to run down the hill and after the four girls and immediately collided with another guard, who shoved a chloroform-soaked rag over her face and a sack over her head.

7

___

DÉJÀ VU – FRIDAY MORNING

The sound of the water lapping against the side of the yacht was familiar. So too was the painful throbbing in her head. She opened her eyes to speckled darkness, not recognising the sack over her head. She closed her eyes assuming she was dreaming. The throbbing was relentless and she involuntarily groaned. She felt hot and sick and couldn't breathe.

'Charlotte,' a voice whispered. The voice was familiar.

'Ayeesha?'

'Yes.'

'Oh Ayeesha. I found you,' she whispered as she fell asleep again.

Someone was pulling her hair.

'Ouch, stop', she cried out. The tugging continued and suddenly the room was awash with light. Blinking rapidly, she scanned the room. Ayeesha was indeed sitting in front of her.

'Here drink this,' she said putting a bottle of water to Charlotte's lips.

'Where am I?'

'We don't know.'

'We?'

A girl leaned forward and said hello. She had an Irish accent.

'You're Niamh?'

'Yes. How'd you know?' the girl whispered excitedly.

'Because Roy's looking for you.'

'Roy's looking for me? Thank God someone is.'

'Hang on to that thought because…I don't think the cavalry will be coming over the hill just yet. We'll need to break out of this prison ourselves.'

'I'm sorry they caught you too. That bloody party. Where the hell is Channing?' Ayeesha asked.

'In Taormina I hope, and on her way back to Kiev. What happened to you on the yacht, Ayeesha?' Ayeesha explained, 'As I was leaving the bathroom, a smart-dressed man smiled at me and leaned in to sniff my neck. I pushed him away and he slapped me yelling, *how dare you*. I punched him back, *hard*, and then it was full-on, with me screaming that I was going to the police. And then someone grabbed me from behind and there was a rag over my mouth and that's all I remember. I woke up here, restrained – in what must be the captain's cabin given the clothes hanging in the wardrobe – with this bro. He was in a much worse state, been in a proper fight with someone.'

'Hello?' Charlotte enquired. A figure was lying motionless in the corner. 'Jacques,' she said softly, 'It's Jack.'

'What? You know him? Is it Jacques or Jack?'

'What did he say?' Charlotte asked.

'He doesn't know who he is. He has concussion and sleeps most of the time. Don't know why they keep him.'

'For ransom. He's from an important and wealthy family.'

'Who is he?'

'Jacques. Jacques Dessault. I met him in Antibes last month. He was working on a yacht. Charming man, somewhat elusive and a rather good kisser.'

'My word, you do know him well,' Ayeesha remarked, with a hint of irony.

'No, no, no. Hardly at all. He just collected something for me. I do know his family is looking for him, though. As indeed your family would be looking for you.'

'Well, no. I doubt it. Niamh tells me that while I was unconscious, they used my thumbprint to access my phone and send a message to my mother. I don't know what the message said or if my mother believed it. She can't afford to fly to Italy to come looking for me. And I don't know where we'll be by the time she realises something serious has happened.' Ayeesha closed her eyes. 'Do you know what they're going to do with us?' Charlotte hesitated before responding. There was no point in hiding the grim reality of their situation.

'I think they make money from slavery as well as gambling and kidnapping.'

'Slavery?'

'That event in Taormina. It was the women who were being sold.' There were at least twenty girls there. All young. All dreaming of a glamorous life.' She turned her attention to Niamh. 'How did they get you?'

'I'm embarrassed because I walked right into their arms. I'd been on a sailing holiday in Corsica. My friends had already left and I missed the last ferry to Nice. No accommodation was available in Ajaccio because the holiday season hadn't officially started.' Niamh shook her head. 'Oldest trick in the book. This guy standing near the tourist information office overheard my conversation and reached out.'.

. . .

Charlotte nodded, and Niamh went on, "I can help you," he said. "We're not officially open, but you're welcome to stay in our hostel. It's a couple of miles back in the hills, but I'm happy to provide a taxi service to and from the port." I couldn't believe my good luck. The *kindly man* helped lift my backpack into the car. It was a new model – something expensive. The doors automatically locked once I was inside, which was unsettling. The hostel was further back in the hills than I'd imagined, and my internet access kept dropping out the further away the car moved from Ajaccio. My worst fears were confirmed when I heard the door lock behind me as I dropped my backpack on the bed in the hostel. They took my phone, made me give a fingerprint and I guess they sent a message to my parents – as they did for Ayeeysha.'

The body in the corner suddenly started thrashing from side to side. Ayeesha placed her hand gently on his wriggling body.

'Jacques. Wake up. You're dreaming.' The body stopped wriggling, and Ayeesha helped him into a sitting position.

'Why did you call me Jacques?'

'Because that's your name'.

'How do you know?'

'Because I told her, Jack. It's Charlotte. You found the bottle with the letter to my brother inside. Do you remember?' He looked at her and said nothing. She continued. 'You took me on a tour of Antibes. It was a small town; you knew it well.' He blinked and looked at the ceiling, trying harder to remember.

'Surely you remember kissing me goodbye,' she said, slightly exasperated. A suggestion of a smile rippled across his face, and then disappeared.

'Your brother died,' he said.

'Yes. My brother died, a long time ago.'

'And you came to get the letter from your parents – all the way from Australia.'

'Yes,' she replied softly.

'And I was, I was...' He sighed. 'Looking for the man who embezzled my family's company, Maurice Morenzo.' Jacques explained what he knew about their captor, telling the women what had led up to his own capture.

'Morenzo worked for my family as directeur financier, or chief financial officer as you call it. He was very good at his job and my father trusted him. One evening at my parents' home, he drank too much and became very familiar with my mother. He started kissing her in the kitchen and she screamed. My father hit him across the head with a lamp and then threw him out. Morenzo was of course instantly dismissed. It was bizarre behaviour that we never understood but were eventually grateful for, because over the next week, as his deputy took over, the extent of his corruption became clear. Not only had he stolen a sizeable sum of money from the business, he'd created taxation problems in several European countries. The discovery would impact on our relationship with our partners, our customers and of course the regulators.

I was furious. I knew he was a clever man and that finding him and bringing him to justice would not be easy. He had many skills and he now had significant financial means. I also knew he had a son who was not so clever. If I could find the son, I could find the father. He'd often spoken proudly of his son Rex, who had experienced great difficulty at school but had found success working as an engineer on yachts.

So I went undercover with one of our yachts, pulling in for repairs at different ports and then asking around for the services of a skilled engineer. We were in the port of Marseilles when I received a response to my request. I was sure it was Rex, but he never turned up for the interview. I waited several hours at the bar and then left. As I was returning to the *Taormina Triumph*, something happened. I heard a noise and then nothing. I woke up with a sack on my head, a blinding migraine and no memory of who I was. Until now.'

'Don't let them know your memory has returned. You'll be a threat if they know,' Charlotte said softly.

TOWARDS MESSINA - THURSDAY AFTERNOON

As the yacht headed out from Naples across the Tyrrhenian Sea for Messina in Sicily, Scott and Roy talked on the bridge.

'Tell me everything you know about the fashion show at the vineyard,' Scott asked.

'Very little I'm afraid. I wasn't a member of the inner circle. Seems to be a big operation with a lot of staff. Principal focus is selling modelling contracts.'

'I have a bad feeling about it.'

'How long will we be in port in Messina?'

'Just short of two days. We leave for Palermo Saturday evening.'

'OK. Let's allay your fears. I've got an idea. I wasn't paid before I unceremoniously left the yacht in Naples. I can go to the Vineyard and demand payment. It's not too far from Messina. Might give me a chance to see Charlotte and to check that she's OK.'

'I'll come with you. Something's definitely amiss. That reference to swimming bothers me. The last time she went in the water she was in serious trouble.'

9

AN INVITATION – FRIDAY EARLY MORNING

Hearing the sound of approaching footsteps, Ayeesha put the sack back on Charlotte's head and retied her own hands as best she could. Rex entered the room, roughly pulled off the sack and dragged Charlotte to her feet.

'Rex. How lovely. Nice to see a friendly face.' She had no idea why she said this. He didn't know how to respond.

'Come,' was all he offered, in a strangely polite way.

She was taken to the upper deck and offered a stool.

'Thanks, Rex,' the Monk said from his position on a swivel, leather chair, several meters away. He was carving himself pieces of an apple with a small knife, staring at her as he did so.

She sat silently, looking quickly around the room, and then back to him. They were alone, and she knew his actions were intentionally menacing.

'Who are you?' he asked softly.

'Charlotte Wyatt.'

'No. Who are you really? Charlotte was confused. 'British Intelligence, BND, Mossad? ASIO?'

'I don't know what you're talking about. I'm a student.'

'Ha,' he chortled. 'Don't take me for a fool. A student alone could not have infiltrated my organisation and caused such disruption.' He sighed. 'I've lost four assets because of you.' Charlotte had no idea what he was talking about. 'We're looking for them now and are confident they'll be retrieved.' Was he talking about the four girls she'd rescued, she thought? And by saying only *four assets were missing* had all the other girls been caught again? Charlotte's spirits sank. She looked at him again and could see that he was regarding her carefully.

'I'm just a student and until recently, a model.'

'With that hairstyle I would assume your modelling opportunities are limited.' A twitch flashed across Charlotte's face. He didn't recognise her. But then why would he? It had been early morning on Ile Sainte Honorat when he had taken her and Scott hostage. It had been very dark. His face was expressionless as he continued to stare at her, pondering his options. Charlotte shivered as he walked slowly towards her, leaned into her face, and took her photo. He then slumped back down into his chair.

'I see you have a significant presence on social media. You were indeed a model.' His thumb rapidly scrolled through the photos. 'I see you get your looks from your mother.' Charlotte squirmed. She was angry at Mason for cajoling her mother into *that* interview, which had been syndicated. Her parents were now at risk. She had no doubt about the ability of The Monk's network to find them and she was afraid. He stopped scrolling and stared at a photo on his screen. Rage washed over his face. He clutched his fruit knife and ran towards her. Charlotte closed her eyes and braced for the pain. Her eyes flew open at the sound of her black trousers being ripped to her thigh and she flinched as the knife carved into her skin several times.

'Curious. Google seems to think that you're also a princess,' he said staring at the scar on her leg. 'You. YOU were the one responsible for the failure of that highly lucrative activity as well.' Charlotte watched him carefully. He placed the knife under her chin forcing her head up. 'What should I do with you? I could kill you. But there's no profit in that. I don't think your family has the means to meet a *reasonable* payment demand. I could of course sell you. With a good haircut, we could obtain quite an attractive price, but your spirited behaviour may mean I need to issue a refund, not too long after the sale. Which of these options would you prefer?' Charlotte considered the pain that each of these choices would cause her parents. She said nothing and could see the pleasure that The Monk was experiencing from her discomfort. 'There may be a fourth option. I need a female member of staff to help me to identify and acquire women for my fashion parades.' Charlotte was horrified. She was being asked to solicit women for his slave trade. 'They are more likely to trust an attractive and *famous* person like yourself.'

Why would he offer me this? Charlotte thought. He must know I'd escape at the first opportunity.

'Of course,' he continued, 'a single infringement, that would in any way negatively impact my business, or an escape attempt would mean your parents would disappear...forever.'

10

THE MONK'S MUSINGS

To say he was rather pleased with himself would be akin to describing coal as black. It was a brilliant idea, although it had risks and he would need to make sure he had a risk mitigation strategy in place. Her family was clearly a point of vulnerability for her. He made a call and knew that he would have the information he needed within the hour to ensure her compliance.

The gala at the vineyard had not been a disaster. Indeed, it had been an opportunity to test the strength of the team and the power of relationships with local authorities. The fire had been quickly extinguished, although a new network blocker needed to be acquired. All of his female assets had been recaptured and the buyers had been reassured that the auction would reconvene shortly. Local media had only reported a fire at a private Breezy concert and that a number of fans had attempted unsuccessfully to gain access. More importantly, Breezy was delighted to confirm that she was unharmed and would give a free concert at the Teatro

Antico di Taormina for her disappointed fans on Saturday night. His phone rang.

'Sì,' He listened carefully. 'Eccellente.'

The Monk was also pleased with his plan for Jacques. He'd given up on the idea of receiving physical cash after the Ile des Lerins disaster and set up a complex arrangement of near instantaneous financial fund transfers through various tax havens. Jacques' parents had wanted confirmation of *proof of life.* He'd refused to let him speak with them, but had sent a photo. Jacques had looked bewildered in the image and his parents had persisted with their request to speak with him. It was unfortunate he did not remember who he was, but in some ways this was to the Monk's advantage, making Jacques a more compliant guest.

His newest *recruit* might be his best acquisition. Charlotte looked so trustworthy, a quality that few of his male employees possessed. It would be interesting to assess how successful she was in recruiting additional 'models'. He'd need to keep a close eye on her to ensure she was contained.

He had not been entirely truthful with her about the four missing girls. They'd been picked up by one of his customers who was in a smaller yacht off the coast, awaiting delivery. His Saudi client had only purchased one girl and he planned to throw in another as a thank you for their quick thinking in collecting his assets. He'd need to arrange for collection of the other two girls on Sunday. For the moment, they were in a safe place – one less thing for him to worry about.

The arrangements for the final auction would need to be communicated to his community of buyers. Most had returned to their villas and hotels in Taormina and Messina when the fire took hold, having planned to be in the area for a number of days to organise shipment of their *goods*. There were a number of ways this was facilitated, from helicopter transfer to yacht and in the back of small goods trucks which appeared to be transporting food through Italy, Croatia, Bosnia Herzegovina and Montenegro all the way to Albania, which was his second major operating hub.

11

CHARLOTTE'S CHOICES

He was playing mind games, leaving her here alone. Testing her. She spotted two cameras set into the ceiling. She was being watched, and one false move would mean the disappearance of the fourth option. To demonstrate vulnerability, she wept a little for the cameras. Her tears however were real. She couldn't stop them once they started. She wept knowing how devastated her parents would be at her disappearance. And she wept because she was angry. Very angry. And if she focussed her anger and her attention then maybe she could escape. Option four it was. Because it would give her time.

'I'm bleeding,' she said matter-of-factly. 'I need antiseptic and bandages.'

'Rex,' The Monk called out. 'We need a supervised visit to the medicine cabinet for our guest.' Slow footsteps down from the bridge announced Rex's arrival. He cut the bindings from her legs and wrists and helped her to stand. Charlotte cried out from the pain and he scooped her up in his arms and carried her down the stairs to a storage room with a large medical cabinet. She was surprised by this chivalrous behaviour. He put her down on a box of canned food and looked at her cuts. He opened the door of the cabinet and retrieved cotton buds, mercurochrome and a selection of plasters and bandages. With surprising care, he tended to the gashes on each leg. While he worked, Charlotte's eyes scanned the contents of the cabinet. The top shelf was full of bottles of Lithium. She wondered who these drugs were for, as she was fairly sure it was used to prevent anxiety attacks for those with bipolar disorders. The storage room also contained large plastic tubs of bottled water, ropes and batteries. Rex completed his nursing duties and helped her to stand. She thanked him and refused his offer to carry her back up the stairs.

The chef placed a tray of cheese and crackers on a small table in front of her. She could read nothing from his expressionless face, but was surprised when he returned moments later with a napkin. With her hands and feet tied up again, there was nothing she could do with the food and she waited for the inevitable return of The Monk.

'Wonderful. Lunch is served.' He reached over and cut her hand ties with his fruit knife. 'Try the gorgonzola. It's one of my favourite cheeses.' She stared at him and didn't move. 'Already suffering from a Judas guilt complex I see. Let me share a story with you.' He looked at his phone and read out loud.

'Melissa Bourne's parents George and Ellen lived in Bangalow. Well, George does still, most of the time, with his second wife Helen Harmon. They also spend a lot of time at her house in Byron Bay.' He looked back at her as her hand flew to her chest. 'You're very fond of your grandparents who, for the moment, are in very good health.' Charlotte's heart raced. 'You're lucky that your father's parents also live in Bangalow. Although strictly speaking, they're not both his parents as Charles Wyatt married Dr Lily McDonald after his first wife Emily died. Your parents of course knew each other growing up, although they went to different schools. They got to know each other better at university, testing their wits during fiery debates. Your father was a bit of a lady's man and had difficulty settling into a relationship. Doesn't appear that he was ever in a relationship with your mother who left Australia for the USA upon completing her studies. Shortly afterwards she met and married Jonathan Brinkley.' The Monk was enjoying revealing what he knew about her family and stopped to sip water for dramatic effect, and to give a sense that there was so much more to come. Charlotte knew her mother had been married before but knew nothing about her first husband, or their relationship.'Your mother and Jonathan lived in Boston, possibly happily, possibly not. It's difficult to confirm as Jonathan died in a car crash while your mother was in Australia. She flew back for the funeral and found out that Jonathan had been in a relationship with someone else who'd also died in the accident. That was it. She'd had enough so sold up and came home. She started working for an interior design company on the Gold Coast while your father was working as a lawyer and making plans to marry Kate in Brisbane.'

Kate who? Charlotte wondered. Doesn't matter, she chastised herself.

'Unbeknown to everyone, your mother was pregnant. The pregnancy was revealed when the baby was born during an emergency caesarean operation following a motor vehicle accident. The baby died the following day. Your father never married Kate, who may have been suicidal, but did marry your mother, three months after your brother Scott's death. You arrived the following year and remain an only child. Your parents live at Kangaroo Point in Brisbane and ...'

'That's enough,' Charlotte snapped. 'Tell me what you need me to do.'

After lunch, Charlotte was locked away from the others in a cabin by herself. The Monk was taking no chances. She spent the hours before sleep engulfed her considering options for rescuing Ayeesha, Niamh, Jacques, the girls at the vineyard and of course herself. At the same time, she also needed to destroy this operation and make sure that The Monk *did not escape*. Her thinking was interrupted by crashing and screaming on the upper deck. She listened carefully and overheard The Monk telling Rex to take his meds. So, the Lithium was his. Charlotte heard Rex walk past her cabin door and she called out to him. The door opened slightly.

'You OK, Rex?' she asked softly. There was an agitated look in his eyes, and he punched the wall hard, bruising and scraping his knuckles.

'Come with me,' Charlotte said with authority, and walked down to the storage room. She passed him two Lithium tablets and a glass of water. As she moved to return the bottle she asked if she could take the mercurochrome, cotton buds and another bandage, showing how the blood had soaked through the bandages that he had applied earlier. He looked at her leg and nodded. She thanked him and compliantly walked back to her room and waited to be locked in. When the footsteps had departed, she put the medical items on the bed and scanned the room for paper. There was none, but she found a cardboard drink coaster on to which she wrote *Don't Drink the Water* using a cotton bud dipped in mercurochrome.

Rex opened her door at first light. He was calmer this morning, so the Lithium had kicked in. She's been up for an hour, 'dressing' her wounds with the bright red mercurochrome so that they looked worse than they were.

'Another bandage, please,' she asked with polite authority and he complied. When Rex went into the storage room to retrieve the bandage, Charlotte pretended to fall, leaning forward and shoved the drink mat under the door of the captain's cabin. Rex came out of the storage room and helped her to stand up. She took the bandage from him and went back to her room to sit on her bed and replace her bandages, wincing frequently while he watched from the door. She then followed him up the stairs to the main deck taking exaggeratedly slow and obviously painful steps. It was better to appear weaker than she was. In effect the cuts had healed well over night. There was a tray with figs and crackers on a small table and a plastic glass of orange juice. She drank the juice and hobbled towards the water dispenser which was one third full. She poured herself a glass and sipped it slowly. Rex had returned to the bridge and for a moment she was on her own. She tipped the dispenser over and poured the crushed lithium tablets into the base of the water distributor before calling out and lying on the floor. Rex, along with another deckhand and The

Monk, came racing in. The deckhand was sent down to the storage room to get another bottle of water for the dispenser and Rex helped her to her feet, and then ran a mop over the floor.

Charlotte nibbled on her crackers and figs while she watched the deckhand replace the water bottle. The Monk picked up a few papers and walked towards her.

'Enough to eat?' It wasn't really a question. 'Get up, Miss Wyatt. You have work to do.'

The helicopter rose slowly from the deck of the yacht. Charlotte watched carefully, wondering if it would be difficult to manoeuvre. She looked down at the sea and the frothy waves which were dancing in the light winds. It was only ten minutes until they touched down at the vineyard, a distance she estimated to be only two kilometres. One of the security guards met the helicopter and helped The Monk to alight. He pulled Charlotte roughly from the aircraft, knowing she was the one who'd stolen his phone and been the source of the fire.

'Gently, gently,' The Monk admonished him. 'She's on our team now.' The guard growled.

'Still, you're right to be concerned. We must make sure someone is with her at all times.'

Charlotte was taken to the ironing room where the elderly woman who gave her the uniform was waiting.

'You stole from me,' she said, as she opened and closed a pair of scissors quickly. Of course. She'd taken the woman's scissors to cut her hair and to cut the girls free. Charlotte said nothing as the woman ran her fingers through Charlotte's unevenly chopped hair. It was intimate and frightening. Her shoulders tightened, not sure what to expect. And then without notice, the woman started cutting her hair. She was getting a makeover and guessed that her recent styling efforts weren't aligned with the image The Monk wished to portray. She sat quietly on the tiny stool and said nothing while the snipping continued, all the while glancing around the room, gathering information and looking for an escape route. There were black marks and dust on the walls. Clearly the fire had made it briefly to this end of the house. Her eyes ran up and down the shelves where the uniforms were stored. Damp and dirty towels were scattered across the floor and had presumably been used to put out the fire. In the corner under one of the towels she could see a black object. It looked like a phone. It could be her phone. Her mind retraced her steps from the previous evening. Yes. She was sure it was hers. A quick change of clothes had been required and her focus had been on getting out and taking the lighter to the control room. The phone must have been left behind with her soiled uniform. In the race to put out the fire, someone had kicked it under the shelving. How could she retrieve it without the woman noticing?

Thirty minutes later the woman announced *finita* and smiled, clearly pleased with her efforts.

'Bella.'

'How would I know?' Charlotte asked. The woman scanned the room and then pointed to the bathroom next door where an ornate mirror hung above the hand basin.

'Yes. Bella,' Charlotte responded with a smile. 'Grazie.' The woman seemed touched by the compliment. Charlotte started dusting off the cut hair with her hands and made exaggerated movements indicating that the cut hair was irritating her. 'Shower please? she asked.

'Come,' the woman commanded. Charlotte followed her back into the ironing room where she was given a towel. She feigned tripping on one of the dirty towels on the floor and was able to kick her phone under the shelving and completely out of sight. She scooped up the dirty towels and placed them in the washing bag, operating as though she was a seasoned member of the team. The woman thought nothing of this gesture and then signalled for her to follow to the room beside the security control centre. Her bag, and the few items of clothing she'd bought in Naples, were spread across the bed. It was clear that the bag had been thoroughly searched. She scooped up the bag and returned to the bathroom. The woman came inside the bathroom, shut the door, and busied herself with cleaning activities while Charlotte showered and changed. Charlotte looked in the mirror and looked at the woman and said thank you again.

'Come,' the woman said, and Charlotte followed her down the hall.

'Un momento,' Charlotte said suddenly, holding the damp towel up and pointing to the ironing room. The woman nodded and Charlotte ducked back in, throwing the towel in the wash basket while scooping up her phone and shoving it down the back of her jeans. She came out shaking her wet hair and nodded at the woman.

The Monk was waiting for them in the entrance to the country house. He raised his eyebrows approvingly as Charlotte approached.

'Bravo, Madre,' he said to the woman. 'She now looks

like Audrey Hepburn in *Roman Holiday*. Perfetta. Perfect.' So, she was his mother, Charlotte noted.

'Good choice of outfit.'

'That's fortunate, as it's the only change of clothes I have.' Charlotte replied. He ignored her comment.

'This is the plan. Luigi will take you into Taormina this afternoon. He will accompany you at all times. You will need to find four suitable candidates. From experience, the best targets are foreign tourists travelling independently. The local girls have too many family members who may come looking for them. Those who have been drinking are easier to persuade. Choose the silly ones. You will start in town around the bars and later attend Breezy's concert at the Teatra Antico di Taormina. Perhaps you can make acquaintances with young girls in the bars that are rekindled later at the concert, it should then be easy to invite them back to the vineyard. You and Luigi will present as cousins.'

'Any questions?'

'How will I pay for drinks?'

'Luigi will pay.'

'And can he buy me a jacket too? I'm cold.' She shivered. He regarded her carefully. 'If Luigi thinks it's suitable then yes. But never forget that I know exactly where your parents are. One misstep and they will be gone.'

Charlotte hated what she had been asked to do. In effect, she was required to befriend young and vulnerable girls and to trick them into a horrible life of debauchery. To make matters worse, they would be sold like cattle at an auction She had to focus. She had to come up with a plan and she had to find a way to get her parents to a safe place, all without attracting the suspicions of Luigi. As she considered her options, she noticed bar staff carrying sacks of bread down the stairs to an area she assumed was the cellar. Of course. The girls had to be kept somewhere, and the cellar was likely to be both large and soundproofed. She wondered how Channing was holding up, indeed how all the girls were managing.

At four o'clock The Monk watched Charlotte and Luigi depart in the minivan for Taormina. He was curious to see how she would perform on her first assignment.

They didn't speak. It was clear that Luigi disliked her.

'Hey Luigi, you'll need to change your attitude, or at least your demeanour, if we're to pull this off. Any woman will be able to tell that you don't like me and will wonder why we're together. You're meant to be my cousin and you're meant to care about me, you'll need to give the impression that you are enjoying my company. Capisci? Do you understand?'

'Do not talk to me like an idiot. I know what I have to do.'

Charlotte did not reply, looking out at the countryside while she considered how she would meet The Monk's challenge.

Luigi chose a public parking station not far from several bars and small shops. As they walked down to the touristy part of town she glanced inside the stores, insisting they stopped each time she saw a coat. Charlotte made a big show of modelling the coats for him.

'What do you think, Luigi?' she asked coquettishly. 'Does it suit my new hairstyle?' He grew increasingly irritated with her and by the sixth store, demanded that she shut up and buy the coat. 'Okeydokey. Credit card please. He stormed out of the store and stood on the pavement watching her take the jacket to the counter to be paid for.

'He's not in a good mood,' the sales assistant observed.

'Agree. He's a miserable bastard. My phone is dead and he has confiscated my charger. Could I buy yours? Add one hundred euros to the bill.'

'Of course, but you have to get away from him. Promise me that.'

'I know. I will.'

'What were you talking to the sales assistant about,' Luigi demanded as she stepped out from the store.

'She didn't like your tone and said that I should leave you.' He seemed surprised by her honesty. 'Look,' she continued, 'this isn't going to work if you don't lighten up. No one will believe me. We need honey to attract bees. You must, we must, be like honey.' He said nothing but his general air indicated that he knew that what she was saying was true.

The first bar they sat down in had walls covered in Mount Etna posters and old empty bottles of liquor. There was nineties music playing through speakers. Locals sat in pairs sipping Campari while nibbling on left over pizza which had been cut into tiny squares. There was a tour group from Scotland, on the last night of a ten-day wine tasting tour of Sicily. They were in good spirits as they relived parts of their tour and occasionally jumped up on to the dance floor.

'Where've you been?' Charlotte asked. They mentioned half a dozen vineyards. 'Sounds wonderful. What was the best bit? The girls went into a huddle arguing over favourite vineyards, attractive men and a ride in a hot air balloon near Palermo.

'Too hard a question,' they laughed.

'And the worst bit?'

'That we have to go home tomorrow,' they chimed together. Everyone hooted and introduced themselves. Charlotte assessed each girl against the criteria The Monk had given her and against her own. She sent Luigi to the bar to buy a round of drinks for the girls.

Isla worked in a call-centre, a job she hated and was looking to escape from. Rowan was a travel agent specialising in adventure tours. Finley had just found her boyfriend in bed with her cousin and needed to get away from everything that reminded her of him. Finley glared at Luigi, who had been introduced as Charlotte's cousin. Mackenzie was a structural engineer and avid triathlon competitor. Paisley spoke six languages and was hoping to get a job as a translator at the United Nations.

'What do you do?' they asked Charlotte. 'I work in marketing and I'm here supporting Breezy.'

'Wow. Lucky girl. Don't s'pose you could get us some tickets?'

'Well yes. Didn't you know she's running a free concert tonight?'

'No. Fab news. Great way to conclude our Sicilian adventure.'

'Starts at eight.'

'And Luigi, what does he do?'

'He works in security.'

'Born for the role I would think,' Rowan offered.

'I agree. Certainly has the demeanour for it,' Finley whispered. Luigi returned with the drinks and Charlotte asked the girls where the bathroom was. She didn't wait to check with Luigi before standing up and entering the door on the left-hand side of the bar. Her phone was dead and there wasn't a power point in the bathroom. There was however one inside the kitchen and she smiled sweetly at the chef, showing him her cable and phone. He waved his hand and Charlotte brought her phone to life. If she was not back in one minute, she knew Luigi would come looking for her. She quickly texted Miranda.

Pls book cabin @ Evans Head 4 week 4 M&D as thnk u present ASAP. More ltr

The phone had 17% battery life left. She turned it off and shoved the cable back in her pocket before bouncing back across the dance floor. Luigi was watching her carefully.

'God, I look a fright. Does anyone have lippy?'

'Shut up. Charlotte. You look great,' Isla said.

'Here.' Paisley passed her a lipstick in a small case with mirror. Charlotte took care applying it to while they all watched.

'Now I'm ready to party. Thanks Paisley.' She passed the lipstick back and turned to Luigi. 'We should get going.' He nodded. 'Lovely to meet you ladies. Might see you later at the concert?'

'You bet,' they chimed in unison.

'Which bar next?' she asked Luigi, and he led the way out onto Corso Umberto.

Two hours later they had visited four bars and spoken with twelve girls. Luigi was relaxing slightly seeing the energetic way that Charlotte was fulfilling her role as *relationship builder*. Announcing he was hungry they stopped at a small pizzeria. After their order had been taken, Luigi left to visit the bathroom. Charlotte quickly scanned the area where she was sitting and found a power point to the side of the booth. She ran the cable down behind the seat and plugged the phone in, making sure to switch it onto airplane mode. Luigi returned as their pizza arrived. Charlotte was hungry, but ate slowly to give her phone maximum time to charge.

'Let's discuss the girls,' she suggested, buying time.

'Pissed-off Isla from the call centre would be my first choice,' Luigi observed.

'Yes, certainly she's looking for a new direction, but I'd be concerned that her father is the Mayor of Glasgow.' Luigi's eyebrows twitched.

'How did you know this?'

'She mentioned it when you were at the bar buying the next round.'

'So, Finley. She'd be my next target.'

'True. She is vulnerable and attractive, but she's a taekwondo master and likely to cause any buyer grief. The other three are better candidates in my view, as well as the two Swedish girls from the last bar.'

'Those Swedish girls looked a bit on the manly side to me.'

'I'm sure our customers have diverse tastes.'

'We only need three girls. We don't need the Swedes.'

'What? Why not?'

'One of our Saudi customers *rescued* all four girls when they waved his yacht down from the beach at the bottom of the vineyard. Curiously, one of the girls, he'd already *purchased*, so it was a convenient collection process. Mr Morenzo is so grateful to Mr Amari that he is throwing another girl in for free. I'll be collecting the other two tomorrow, so we only need to acquire three girls to clean up your slate.' Charlotte's heart sank. She thought she'd saved them. 'We've gotta go. Get up.'

'I'm thirsty, can you buy a bottle of water when you pay the bill?' Luigi did as instructed and went up to the bar, giving Charlotte precious seconds to unplug the phone and place it with the cable in her coat pocket. She stood and sauntered over to the bar to join him.

12

BREEZY CONCERT – FRIDAY 7:30PM

They caught a taxi from the car park, which was some distance away from the Teatro Antico di Taormina. As they walked the last part of the way to the theatre, they were surrounded by hundreds of Breezy fans, including a number of girls that they had already met in the bars that afternoon. They exchanged excited dancing movements and propositions they catch up for another drink after the show. There were thumbs up all round.

'Charlotte, what a surprise to see you here.' The female voice was familiar. Charlotte turned around.

'I could say the same for you, Teal.' Charlotte shook hands with the immaculately coiffured woman. She was genuinely astonished to see the international treaties expert that she'd met at the party on the yacht in Rome, here in Taormina.

'My word, that was a wonderful party. I'd like to write to the host to thank them and I'm embarrassed that I don't know who that was.'

'Luigi here will be able to help you. He works for the same company.' Luigi was momentarily lost for words.

'We have an office in Rome. You could send the thank you letter there.'

'Wonderful. Could you give me the address?' Luigi regarded her carefully then started tapping on his phone.

'You know, Charlotte, I could really help you with my contacts for fabrics.' This woman, who'd she'd only met once, knew she was in trouble and was offering help.

'That's so generous of you, Teal. I can't accept help for the moment as I've taken another position for the foreseeable future.'

'Of course.'

'But who knows, maybe I'll follow through on my fashion design idea and come back to you for help. Not only with fabrics, but also fasteners and zips.'

'Here's the address,' Luigi said, thrusting the screen of his phone towards Teal. She took a photo of the post box address and thanked him.

'Great. Well, I'll be off. Hoping to score a Breezy autograph.'

'She's old to be a Breezy fan,' Luigi observed wryly.

'She's not that old,' Charlotte retorted.

Charlotte and Luigi took a seat in the last row on the far aisle on the left. Luigi left Charlotte for a few minutes to go to the bathroom again, so she quickly checked her phone's messages.

Thanks for Evans Head gift voucher. Hope you'll be able to take a break from your studies next month to join us. ❤*Mum & Dad*

. . .

'Damn,' she cursed. 'They need to go immediately.' She read Scott's message. So he was in Taormina too. So much she wanted to say to him. Too big a risk. So little time. She could see Luigi on his way back from the bathroom, so she leant over coughing and quickly texted.

Pls get M & D to EH ASAP. ☠

She turned her phone off and surreptitiously slipped it back into her pocket. The three Scottish girls they'd chatted with earlier, called out from the other side of the venue and Charlotte pointed to the three seats that were free in front of them.

'Where's Isla and Finley?' Charlotte asked.

'Mt Etna's puffing so they've opted for a night tour of a potentially exploding volcano.' Mackenzie explained. 'Very tempting, but we'd rather be here.'

'Thought you'd have a *golden pass* and be sitting down the front?' Rowan commented as they took their seats.

'We've heard her before,' Charlotte replied with a grin. 'And something to think about. There's going to be an after-concert party at a vineyard up the road. Let me know if you're interested but you must keep this news to yourself – numbers are limited.'

'Did you hear that ladies,' Rowan called out to her friends. 'Would we be open to attending a private party with Breezy?'

'I'm a bit busy, but I could squeeze it in,' Mackenzie offered.

'Oh. OK then. If we must,' Paisley added, shaking her head in disbelief.

. . .

Breezy walked on to the stage and the crowd rose to their feet cheering and clapping.

'Hello Taormina. Wonderful to be here in this beautiful theatre on this lovely evening. How are you?' The crowd roared and Breezy turned to her band, started clicking her fingers and said, 'One, two, three.'

Charlotte stood up, as all the other fans were doing, and danced along to a string of Breezy's most popular songs. Luigi looked out of place as he stood miserably among the bopping girls. As she danced, she scanned the crowd and saw Scott and Roy on the other side of the theatre with their hands above their heads, waving at her. She raised her hands too, as though waving along to the music while vigorously shaking her head. They put their hands down and she started clapping her hands high in the air. Phew. They'd got the message.

'Let's go down the front to dance,' Paisley shouted above the din. 'There's more room.' Before Charlotte had time to obtain Luigi's permission, the girls had dragged her down to an area in front of the band. She turned back to Luigi and shrugged her shoulders as she followed them down the steps. They jived, they bumped and sang out loud. Charlotte loved that she was now a member of this Scottish clique.

'OK people. It's time to go,' Breezy announced.

'Nooo,' came a collective cry from the audience.

'Afraid so. Well, why don't we have one last song. A new one from my lead guitarist Rob. Ladies, I'd like you to clear this area here. This song is a slow burner. It's a song of regret. An ode to the things we didn't say.' Gentle clapping was followed by silence as the crowd listened intently to the opening chords played on a single guitar. It was a song for slow dancing. Charlotte felt someone grab her hand. It was Scott. Before she could say anything, he's pulled her to the centre of the dance floor, put his arms around her waist and pulled her close.

'I think you should reciprocate. We're on display.' Charlotte leaned in, wrapped her arms around his neck and started swaying to the music. She grimaced as he sang along to the song's chorus.

'What do you need me to do Charlie Girl?' he whispered in her ear.

'Get my parents to safety.'

'But what about you? If you're in trouble, we can leave now and go to the police.'

'No. Don't. Too risky. Some police are involved with this mafia mob.' At that moment, Scott swung her out wide before pulling her back in closer. He stared into her eyes before leaning in again.'

'Is there anything I can do?'

Charlotte described the four girls being held captive by the Saudi businessman, on his yacht, not far from the vineyard. 'They'll be collected very soon.'

'Anything else?'

'Tell Roy that Niamh is OK. I'm working on breaking her out,' He looked at her in awe, then kissed her. It was so lovely, but she knew that Luigi would be watching and fuming She broke from the kiss and slapped him hard across the face before storming up the steps.

'What did he say to you,' Luigi demanded as she retook her place.

'Nothing I care to repeat. Men are pigs. The girls are coming now. Let's leave. Go get the van and we'll meet you at the gate.' Charlotte was a little surprised that he responded to her demands so compliantly.

The three girls regarded her curiously as they came up the steps.

'We're guessing he didn't get an invite to the after-party surprise?'

'You're right there, Paisley.'

'He was kinda cute. You could have passed your castoffs our way.'

'I wouldn't worry. You may see him again soon.'

'I saw him first. I've got dibs,' Mackenzie shouted, and the other girls laughed.

13
____

FOUR HOURS EARLIER

The vineyard was located between Messina and Taormina. The guard let Roy walk up to the large house somewhat reluctantly, refusing to let Scott accompany him. Scott cooled his heels near the taxi, and examined the route Charlotte's phone had taken the previous evening. The signal had stopped several hours ago, with the last location being in the house. He could only speculate as to whether the phone had been shut down or run out of power.

The door was opened by one of the crew from the *Paradiso* who showed Roy to the accountant's room. The scent of fire immediately filled his nostrils, but he could see little damage. He was instructed to sit while the accountant opened the safe to withdraw cash, and update the online payroll record system. Roy was then instructed to sign a form acknowledging receipt of funds. He scribbled his name and his eyes flickered to a pile of folders on the corner of the desk. On the top of the pile was a folder with the name Channing Koval in large print and a stamp of

Venduta: SOLD. The accountant stood and pointed his finger at the door.

'Grazie,' Roy said politely as he left and walked slowly towards the entrance. He could see no sign of Channing or any other young women. An older woman was sweeping the terrace of black ash, there were repairs being made to roof tiles and there were chairs being removed from one of three large marquees on the lawn. He considered wandering down to investigate but the woman who was sweeping had stopped, and was now staring at him. He waved at her, exited through the heavy wooden doors, and walked slowly down to the taxi, where Scott was waiting impatiently.

'Anything?' Scott asked. Roy was biting his lip and frowning.

'I couldn't see her. Well, any girls for that matter. Maybe they've all gone now the event is over. It was quiet in the house. But what worries me is what has been *sold*.' Roy described what he had seen on the cover of the folder. 'Something has been sold. Perhaps it's just a modelling service. Perhaps it's something like, ...'

'Trafficking. They could have been sold as slaves,' Scott finished his sentence.

'Hard to get my head around,' Roy replied looking nervously back towards the house.

'Charlotte was definitely here.' Scott turned on his app to look at the circuitous route her phone had taken around the vineyard on the previous evening and was startled when a single ping from her phone appeared and then disappeared. Scott clapped his hands, tipped his head back and closed his eyes. 'She's in Taormina, at a bar.'

'Thank God for that.' He hit her number and tried to call. Voicemail.

· · ·

OK Charlie Girl. Just checking in that you're OK. Call me. Please.

'Feel like a drink, Roy?'

'You bet.'

'Taormina please,' Scott instructed the taxi driver.

The bar was crowded, very crowded. Roy ordered drinks while Scott tried again to call Charlotte.

It's me. Just checking in to see if you need rescuing. I'm in Taormina. Call me. Or text me. Or send a carrier pigeon

'The barman said she might have been here. They had a lot of giggly girl tour groups earlier.'

'She's not really the giggly type,' Scott replied. He opened a browser and googled 'fire Taormina'. A single result came back that he feed through the translator.

Small fire at Vittoria d'oro Vineyard quickly extinguished Friday night revealing private concert by pop singer Breezy.

'Pity there's no photos.'

'Who says there's no photos. Go on. Google "Breezy concert",' Roy said. Scott's thumbs furiously tapped the screen.

'You're right mate. There's a couple here on Insta. All a bit fuzzy and all taken by Channing Koval.' Scott enlarged the photos but couldn't recognise anyone apart from Breezy. He shook his head and bit his lower lip. 'Breezy was at the vineyard,' he said factually, testing his disbelief.

'And she's playing at the Teatro Antico tonight if you're interested,' the waiter said as he placed the beers on their table. He was pleased to use his English and to share the exciting news. 'It's free and open to everyone.'

'You been working here all afternoon?' The waiter nodded. 'Do you recognise this person?' he said holding up his phone with a photo of Charlotte taken when she was modelling in Central Park, New York.

'Well, she certainly didn't look like that today, but yes, she was here. She used the power point in the kitchen to charge her phone.'

'How did she appear to you?'

'Fine. Nothing remarkable. Why don't you find out yourself? I'd be surprised if she wasn't going to the concert.'

'Thank you. Let's go mate.' They buttoned their coats and Scott's phone pinged. He picked it up expectantly hoping for a message from Charlotte. Instead, it was a message from his sister Miranda.

Why does Charlotte want her folks to go to Evans Head immediately?

Don't know. Will find out.

The taxi dropped Scott and Roy not far from the entrance to the theatre and they filed in, scanning the crowd for Charlotte.

'Let's go down the front so we can better see everyone's faces.' This was easier said than done, as they squeezed their way down the steps through throngs of excitable fans. There was an even split of Italian fans and foreign holiday makers keen to take in the music and views from the wonderful, historic location.

'There she is,' Roy, said suddenly pointing to the far side of the theatre. She was chatting with a couple of girls and had a miserable looking, curly-haired bloke to her side. They started waving at her. She saw them, looked horrified and sent a clear signal back to stop waving.

'What the hell is that all about? And who's that bloke she's with?'

'I think he's a member of the security team from the *Paradiso*.'

'Then she's in trouble.' Scott examined her most recent text message. 'This message made no sense. I need to talk to her without getting in the face of that mafia mobster.'

'I think you're right.' Roy nodded.

'About what?'

'I think he's connected to the mafia and that they're holding something over her, or she's really upset with you after your last conversation.' Scott playfully punched his friend in the arm. 'So, which one is it lad?'

'Well, our last conversation was in her hotel room in Rome.'

'Do I need to hear any more of this?'

Scott sighed and rolled his eyes. 'I was imploring her to promise to keep out of trouble.'

'And her response?'

'Wouldn't make the commitment.'

'Anything else?' Scott remembered the taste of her as he kissed her. He remembered wanting to stay to see where the kiss led, but needing to go. A smile flickered across his face. 'Nope. Nothing else. She must be in with the mafia.'

Scott watched her intently, afraid she might disappear at any moment, while Roy bopped along to the music with all the other Breezy fans enjoying the concert. Scott could see Charlotte chatting with the girls in the row in front, and when they encouraged her to come down to the area in front of the stage, he knew this might be his only chance to talk with her. Without advising Roy of his plan, he pushed through the crowds, grabbed her hand and pulled her on to the dance floor. For dramatic effect, he sang along to the chorus,

'I didn't know I loved you, until you went away, with a hole in my heart I've come to regret, the things I didn't say,'

He then pulled her close and whispered the questions he needed answered. He was stunned by her reply and request. His heart ached at her predicament and without thinking, he leaned in and kissed her. The force of her slap surprised him. He put his hand to his face, continuing the very public theatre, while watching her storm up the stairs.

'OK then laddie. Must have been number two. You must have really pissed her off in Rome?' Roy said with a grin.

'You don't know the half of it mate. Come. We've work to do.'

'Can't we wait for a moment in case there's an encore?'

'Charlotte's seen Niamh.' Roy gasped and followed Scott as they pushed their way out through the crowd…

14

REALITY TV OPPORTUNITY – FRIDAY
10:00PM

Dark storm clouds gathered overhead as they waited for Luigi to arrive with the minivan.

'I've got an idea to run past you girls. Are you interested in earning something extra for your next holiday?' 'How much time would it take? We've got flights booked back home tomorrow evening.'

'Couple of hours. Three tops.'

'We're in. What's involved?'

'An Australian network is filming a reality tv show that's a cross between *Big Brother* and *The Hunger Games*. There are a dozen girls being kept prisoner in the basement of the vineyard, in preparation for an auction where they will be sold as slaves to buyers from the Middle East.'

'You weren't kidding. That's incredibly dark.'

'Your mission, should you choose to accept it, is to engineer a breakout. You each have different skills, as do the girls already playing the game. Some of the girls in the basement already feel the situation is hopeless and have stopped trying to escape. You need to reenergise them. Be aware that there are cameras everywhere, and you must stay in role, playing along with each scenario as it's presented to you.'

'And what's the prize?'

'It's travel related.'

'Yeah. I'm in,' Rowan announced.

'Me too,' Paisley and Mackenzie chimed in unison.

'Great. I'll give you more details once we get there.'

'What a lovely cottage,' Rowan remarked as the minivan bumped its way up the pot-holed road to the front door.

'Kind of spooky,' Mackenzie replied.

'Ooh. I think it's a wonderful location for ...' Paisley caught herself, remembering that she was meant to be *in role*. Charlotte had to remind herself that she too was *in a role* as a newly recruited member of the The Monk's Mob.

Luigi opened the door and Charlotte directed the girls to follow her, discreetly pointing at the cameras that were filming the reality TV show.

One of the security men came over as though to apprehend the girls.

'No, I've got this Marco,' Charlotte said with authority. 'Give me the keys.' He hesitated before placing them in her open palm. As the girls descended the narrow steps to the basement, Charlotte turned. 'Don't forget the assessment criteria. Work as a team. Employ creative thinking in identifying ways to escape and never, ever give up.' The girls smirked, excited by the challenge. Charlotte momentarily struggled with the keys to the cellar, before opening the door into the darkness. As the girls filed past her, Charlotte whispered in Paisley's ear, 'Camera on your left. Best of luck. See you on the other side.' As she closed the door, she heard a distressed Channing call out, 'Charlotte. Come back. Don't leave us.' Turning the key, she caught her breath and remounted the stairs.

'I'll take those,' Luigi demanded as she reached the top. She dropped them in his open palm and continued to the next staircase. 'And you're going where?'

'The bathroom,' she replied without turning around. Out of sight of her captors. she turned her phone on. No signal. Damn. Those blockers must have been restored. She placed her phone and cable behind the old cistern and flushed the toilet.

'Goodness,' she cried out as she walked into Mr Morenzo who was waiting immediately outside the bathroom door. He leant forward and patted her down.

'You're coming with me. There's a problem on the yacht.'

'Of course,' she replied, wondering exactly what had transpired while she'd been away.

15

JACQUES: SIX HOURS EARLIER ON THE PARADISO

The message on the drink mat raised so many questions. It must be from Charlotte. What was she planning? They needed to wait.

Several hours after they heard the helicopter depart, they could hear gentle moaning from the nearest bathroom. The crew member who brought their lunch looked sleepy and they could hear a violent argument between Rex and the chef about the contents of the previous evening's meal. No one remembered to collect their trays or retie their hands. Working quickly together, they escaped their bindings. Jacques used the end of a teaspoon to remove the screws from the door and looked out into the corridor. It was empty. He raced to the storeroom to collect several metres of rope that he passed to the girls while grabbing a battery, the only item he could feasibly use as a weapon. It was eerily quiet. He poked his head into the crew bunk room. Two men were in a coma-like sleep. They quickly bound their legs and arms to the bed with the rope. Their prisoners barely murmured.

The chef was slouched on a chair in the kitchen, with an

ice-pack on his head. He'd clearly sustained a head wound in his disagreement with Rex.

'Bandage,' Jacques whispered to Niamh. She retraced her steps to the storage room and grabbed a bandage from the cabinet. As she was about to leave, she heard unsteady footsteps in the corridor. She ducked behind the rack of water bottles in the corner. Rex was clearly in a foul mood as he counted the small bottles on the top shelf of the medicine cabinet.

'Argh,' he screamed. 'That girl must go.' Niamh waited until she could hear that he'd made his way up to the bridge, before scooting down the corridor to the kitchen. The chef was secured on a seat and they quickly wrapped the bandage around his bloodied head.

It was agreed that Niamh and Jacques would work together to secure Rex and the bridge, while Ayeesha would go below to ready the jet skis in case escape vehicles were needed.

Jacques overheard Rex tell his father there was a 'problema dell'acqua' as he tiptoed into the bridge. The helicopter was visible on the horizon and Jacques knew that their arrival was only minutes away. He watched in horror as the door of the helicopter opened and Charlotte was pushed out.

16

CHARLOTTE: TEN MINUTES EARLIER

As they walked to the helicopter pad, Charlotte noticed that there were now only two marquees, located close together. She assumed that one was for the auction and the other for processing. Many of the buyers from the previous evening had returned, and were standing on the lawn drinking. The man who'd given her the cigarette lighter spat on the ground and glared at her with disgust.

The helicopter was soon in the air and Charlotte could see the path from the grounds of the stone house through the vineyards, over several hills and down to a small beach. As they flew across the sea the radio crackled. It was the unmistakable voice of Rex telling his father that she had put his Lithium in the water tank. The Monk unbuckled his seat belt and reached across to unbuckle hers.

'I told you that disobedience would not be tolerated.' He opened her door and shoved her out. 'And your parents will be the next ones to die,' he shouted after her.

Charlotte grabbed the skids with both arms as the pilot attempted to shake her off with a sweeping motion. The

Monk then started stamping on her hands. She hung on defiantly until he pulled his gun and pointed it at her head. There was nothing else to do but let go. The buttons on her new coat flew off and she grabbed the sides, which were wildly flapping in the downward draft, and was able to create a parachute effect for a few precious seconds before she hit the water. Hard. She was familiar with the feeling and did not panic as she sunk further and further. The sea floor arrived sooner than expected and she went down into a crouch before pushing herself up for the surface, removing the heavy coat which had reduced the speed of her descent, but was making it hard to push for the surface. She could see the moon as she crawled upwards and it gave her hope. Breaking the surface, shivering, she took several deep breaths of the gorgeous air. Her entry into the water had hurt. While her face felt like it had been slapped with a whip, she knew she'd broken no bones in the fall. The lights of houses were sprinkled on the distant hills. They were her true north. She rolled onto her front and began the stroke she'd used many times to swim for shore.

She'd halved the distance to the nearest beach when she heard the familiar buzz of an approaching jet ski. She took a deep breath and ducked down below the water's surface. The jet skier was doing figure-eights and using a torch to look for her. As the vessel moved further away Charlotte slowly resurfaced and was delighted to hear a familiar voice.

'It's me. Ayeesha. I'm here to rescue you.'

'It's about time,' Charlotte called out, slapping the water to indicate her location.

Ayeesha pulled her up behind her.

'Where to?'

Charlotte pointed to a small beach five hundred metres ahead. 'We have a castle to storm.'

It was easy to find the path from the beach, back over the hills and through the vineyards to the edge of the grounds hosting the marquees. They covered the distance in ten minutes. There was no sentry on duty at the *pissing corner*, so Charlotte marched Ayeesha directly to the house.

'Leave me alone, you bitch,' Ayeesha cried out as they walked into the spotlights surrounding the house.

'What's this?' Luigi demanded.

'An escaped asset. Include her on the auction list. She'll add a bit of colour.' Charlotte pushed Ayeesha forward towards the house.

'Do you have the keys?'

With Ayeesha now amongst the other girls, Charlotte dusted off her hands.

'I need to change,' she said matter-of-factly to Luigi and walked inside the house. She was staggered that he didn't challenge her. The Monk's mother was walking slowly down the stairs with a basket full of clothes. She stopped and stared. Charlotte nodded to acknowledge her and continued up to the ironing room. With a dry uniform in hand, she slipped into the bathroom and locked the door.

Damn. Her phone was gone. Who had it? Still, no one had stopped her, and they seemed to have accepted, if rather begrudgingly, that she was now a member of the team. She showered quickly, dressed, and tidied her hair before joining the evening's guests in the large marquee.

17

JACQUES: THIRTY MINUTES EARLIER ON THE PARADISO

Nooo,' Jacques screamed as he saw Charlotte struggling to hang on to the landing gear of the helicopter. Rex turned around and sneered. The pilot was dipping and diving with the machine in an attempt to shake her off. Horrified he watched as Maurice Morenzo stamped on her arms, and then drew his gun before she let go.

'Not able to save your damsel in distress today?' Jacques hit Rex hard with all the anger of the last month's confinement. Rex fell to the floor, unconscious, and Niamh quickly secured him with ropes.

From the security cameras on the bridge, Jacques and Niamh watched the helicopter land and the pilot and The Monk disembark. Both were heavily armed. Niamh slipped downstairs while Jacques picked up the flare gun.

Niamh broke the light in the kitchen, set her trap and hid in the cold-room. She could hear heavy steps approaching. The moonlight allowed the pilot to see the chef sitting on a chair in the kitchen.

'Claude,' he called out. 'Are you OK?' There was no

response from the unconscious man. The pilot walked towards him and slipped on the floor, which had been covered in cooking oil. He struggled to maintain his balance and then fell awkwardly, hitting his head against a table. As he hit the ground his gun discharged and shot him in the foot. He screamed out in pain. Niamh emerged from her hiding place, kicked the gun into the corner and tied up his hands. Confident that he was secure, she picked up the gun and crept back up the steps to the bridge.

'You're trespassing on my boat,' Jacques hissed.

'So, the boy's memory has returned. Good for you.'

'I hope you have many memories, Maurice, as that is all you will have to keep you company for your life in jail.'

'Your arrogance. This is why I despised your family. Well – apart from your mother.'

They both heard the gun go off in the kitchen, which acted like a trigger as Jacques lunged at his nemesis' throat. The Monk dropped his gun as he worked hard to remove the steel-like fingers crushing his neck. Another gun shot went off, shattering the glass of a side window and the men turned to look at Niamh, who now had possession of both guns, which were pointing at them.

'Tie him up,' she instructed Jacques, kicking the rope towards him. 'Sorry about the damage to your Dad's boat.'

18

THE SCOTS PLAY THE GAME – FRIDAY 11:30PM

It smelt of fear inside the basement. The other girls regarded them carefully as they took in the environment of their *Big Brother* home.

Paisley introduced herself. 'What are your names?' she asked in English, Italian and Arabic, eliciting a response from all the girls. Melba, Karin, Stella, Marie, Channing, Anna, Martina, Alice, Georgia, Yana, Khrystyna and Noor.

'Anyone else having signal problems?' Mackenzie asked while she rebooted her phone.

'There's a signal blocker. It's not possible to access the internet,' Channing said.

'Cor. They're making this game difficult.'

'What game?' Channing asked incredulously. Mackenzie remembered that the rules of their participation were that they needed to remain in role as prisoners, until they had escaped.

'The game is to get out of here. Tell me, what have you tried already?'

'It's impossible to escape. The only exit is through that door.'

'So, what have you tried?'

'The walls are made of stone and the two windows are barred.'

'Again. What have you tried?' Mackenzie said, exasperated. 'Can we dig our way out?'

'Though stone? Not possible,' Stella said.

'Are any of the window bars weak?' Mackenzie suggested. Channing ran to both windows, pushed open the shutters and attempted to shake the iron bars.

'No, it's not possible,' she cried.

'You're not thinking creatively. What about the ceiling?' Mackenzie went into the bathroom and stood on the toilet. She was tall, but needed another metre of height to reach the bathroom ceiling.

'What if I got on your shoulders?' Channing suggested.

'That's the thinking. Come and shut the door behind you.'

It was relatively easy to remove the fan, although the plaster required force. There was a timber floor above and it took a few minutes to remove three of the loosest planks.

'I need help,' Mackenzie called out in a staged whisper through the bathroom door. Stella scurried to the bathroom and helped push Channing up through the ceiling.

Channing swung her feet up into small room with buckets, mops and brooms.

'I'm here. What's the plan?'

'Create a distraction while I get everybody else out,'

'Got it,' Channing said confidently, with no idea as to how she would achieve this. She peeked outside the broom closet, listening carefully for sounds of others. There were people chatting in a room down the end of a corridor. She slipped into the nearest room which was a bathroom. As she opened the window, she noticed a phone stuck behind the cistern. She put it in her pocket and climbed out onto the roof. One of the tiles rattled under her feet and she dropped to her knees and held her breath. Silence. No one had noticed. She put the phone inside her jumper and turned it on so that the light did not attract attention. The Australian flag made it easily identifiable as Charlotte's phone. She remembered her password, too, as Charlotte had let her take photos with Ayeesha when they were on the yacht in Rome.

Channing scanned the area around the house while she carefully dislodged a roof tile. She threw it like a discus towards the main marquee, easily piercing the canvas, and landing on someone inside. Screams of distress disturbed the quiet evening and guests ran out from the tent, like ants escaping a flooded nest. Channing then hit the play button on the music app of Charlotte's phone and a distinctive riff from Led Zeppelin added to the pandemonium. The phone was thrown into the middle of a rose garden at the front of the house. She lay down on the tiles and took deep breaths to still her racing heart. After ten seconds the music stopped as the phone's battery died, but it had had the desired effect as the Monk's men swarmed the grounds looking for the source. There were screams inside the house and she could hear several girls being restrained. Damn. She desperately hoped that some had got away. The distinctive click of a Glock instinctively made her close her eyes.

'There are two ways off this roof. You come back through the bathroom window or you jump.'

Channing took the first option and Luigi shoved her with brute force back into the basement and slammed the door shut. Mackenzie helped her to get back to her feet. The distinctive sounds of hammering above revealed that repairs were being made to ensure that route was no longer an option.

'Well done.'

'So how many girls escaped?'

'Four, but all recaptured,'

'So disappointing.'

'No. You're wrong. Look around the room. The girls are inspired. Success in breaking out has given them confidence.' Indeed, the girls were animated. Mackenzie invited them to come closer, and with Paisley's translation assistance, asked them all what they'd learnt and what lessons could be applied for the next attempt. The distinctive sound of keys in the padlock, prompted a shush from Rowan as all eyes turned to the door. Someone was cursing and resisting being handled. A woman of African origin was thrown to the floor. She quickly sprang to her feet and spat at her gaoler. Charlotte wiped the spit from her face unmoved, turned, and instructed Luigi to lock the door behind her.

AYEESHA'S MOMENT – FRIDAY 11:45PM

'My god. Was that Charlotte?' Channing cried out in disbelief.

Ayeesha stood up, shook off the ropes gently binding her hands and grinned.

'How's everyone keeping?' The girls smiled with relief.

'Disappointed that the first escape attempt had failed. But very motivated to try again,' Mackenzie replied.

'Good news. I've brought along a few things which might help.' Ayeesha pulled from her pocket the small tool kit she'd retrieved from the jet ski. The group examined each item and then huddled together, sharing ideas until the sound of the now familiar key in the lock, forced them to spread apart and be silent.

'It's time to get ready for the parade,' Luigi announced. The Monk's mother followed him in with the basket of clothes. 'In a line behind this person now,' he demanded putting his hand on Stella's head. She flicked it off with annoyance and he hit her across the face. The girls immediately started lining up behind Stella. Satisfied that they were complying, Luigi grunted and left, locking the door behind him. Ayeesha and Mackenzie took a place at the end of the line with Paisley, Channing and Rowan.

'You know,' Ayeesha said softly, 'we've just been given a gift. Charlotte told me that that the old woman was the mother of the mafia boss Morenzo. We just need to apply some alternate thinking. If we change our perspective from breaking out of here, to making sure no one could break in, then...' She leant forward and outlined her idea. Channing looked up and saw that Stella was now wearing a thigh-length, one-shouldered tunic in a style worn by Egyptian slaves. There certainly was no subtlety in the image she presented.

'How are you, honey? Let me look at your face.' Channing pulled the still shocked Stella over to the door where the light was better and looked at the swelling on her cheek. Rowan joined them, giving Stella a hug before moving behind her to secure the door using cable ties from the tool kit. Paisley moved quietly to the end of the room and did the same thing with the bathroom door. With the fortress in place, they surrounded the Monk's mother and quickly contained her.

'Now what?' Channing asked Ayeesha.

'Get out of those demeaning rags, girls.'

There was a frisson among the girls, indeed a thrill, as they awaited their gaolers' return. They didn't have to wait long. Fifteen minutes later they could hear Luigi's feet slowly descending the stone stairs. He unlocked the padlock and leaned against the door. It didn't move. Surprised, he pushed it harder with his shoulder. There was initial confusion followed by shouts of anger, as he rattled the door.

'Stop,' Channing commanded. 'We have a piece of

broken glass to the throat of Mrs Morenzo. We are desperate women, and we have no compunction in slitting her throat. We suggest you move away from the door and ask Mr Morenzo if he would like to see his mother alive again.'

'What's going on?' Luigi demanded.

'You heard me correctly. We are secured inside and so is Mr Morenzo's mother. She is our prisoner and will not be released until we're given our freedom.'

'Marco, I need help. Over here NOW! Charlotte Wyatt. What the hell is this?'

'I've no idea what you're talking about,' Charlotte replied innocently.

'The girls have taken Mama Morenzo hostage.'

'And who let Mrs Morenzo into the basement on her own?' Luigi knew that this lapse of security was his failing. He hesitated for a moment and then pulled out his phone to call the Monk. It went through to voicemail.

'We have a situation, sir. Please call me back.' Luigi anxiously massaged his temples with his forefingers.

'Excuse me,' one of the bar staff said, interrupting his thoughts.

'Sì. Yes?'

'We have guests at the front door.'

'What? Then invite them down to the marquee.'

'I don't think they're buyers.' Luigi shook his head.

'Are you sure?'

'Yes.'

'Come with me,' he said grabbing Charlotte roughly by the arm.

Charlotte was as surprised as Luigi to see Breezy standing in the foyer with six very muscly women.

'So. Where are you hosting my party? Hope you've got plenty of chairs. There's three cars full of fans following us.' Charlotte smiled. The cavalry was coming.

'Of course. Welcome. And well done on a fantastic concert,' Charlotte offered enthusiastically.

'Yes. I could see you bopping away down the front.'

'We have chairs on the terrace. Make yourself comfortable while I rustle up refreshments.' She raised her hand, and clicked her thumb and finger attracting the attention of the head waiter. 'Andrea,' she called out with confidence, 'champagne needed over here please. Pronto.'

Luigi was overwhelmed, realising that his options were narrowing by the minute. It was a disaster and he would pay a heavy price when Morenzo returned. He walked down to the cellar and unlocked the door. He didn't wait to check on the condition of Mrs Morenzo, instead walking directly over to the main marquee to where their guests were sitting expectantly. He explained that the auction had been delayed and that it was in their best interests to leave the property now. The meaning in this message was immediately understood, as the men walked quickly and then ran to their cars. With so many assets lost, Luigi knew that he needed to retrieve the girls the Saudi businessman was holding on his yacht. He signalled to Marco that they had a job to do, leaving the vineyard devoid of leadership.

Charlotte welcomed each girl as they emerged from the basement and directed them to the terrace where drinks and canapes were being served.

'How'd we do?' Mackenzie asked as she high-fived Charlotte on the way up the stairs.

'I'm waiting on the judges final remarks, but I was pretty impressed. You should be very proud of yourselves.'

'Breezy, you're here!' Rowan called out. 'I'm your biggest fan. That was such an awesome concert.'

'You're so kind,' the singer replied humbly.

Channing was the last girl out of the basement.

'I don't know what happened tonight. My head is spinning. You are trully remarkable whoever you are.'

'I'm just Charlotte.'

'Well *just-Charlotte,* thank you. And if you're looking for your phone, you'll find it in the front rose garden. And Charlotte?'

'Yes, Channing?'

'Led Zeppelin? Really? You're always surprising me.' Charlotte smiled and left to retrieve her phone.

'Well ladies,' Breezy commented lifting up her champagne glass, 'thank you for coming to my concert and congratulations on winning your very challenging game. Ah – what was it called again?'

'Roman Roulette,' Charlotte replied with the smallest of grins.

Messina, Saturday morning 2:00am

Charlotte had to gently wake the girls as they arrived at the Europa Palace Hotel in Messina an hour later. It had been an added treat to travel in Breezy's tour bus. As each girl exited the bus, Teal Dubois asked for their name and nationality and gave them a hotel room keycard.

'Breakfast is from 7:00am where I'll explain your travel arrangements for getting home.' Charlotte was last off the bus, save for Breezy and her dance crew who remained aboard, undoubtedly headed for more luxurious accommodation.

'Why am I not surprised to see you here?' she remarked matter-of-factly to this curious woman from the embassy.

'It's clear that I'm not the only one with multiple roles and talents.' Teal leaned into the bus, called out thanks to Breezy and offered a wave of thanks to the crew and driver.

'Anytime honey,' Breezy replied. And the bus left.

'Here's your key, Miss Wyatt. We should talk more tomorrow.'

'Sure. A question for you.'

'Bien sûr. Of course.'

'Were those Amazonian-like women really Breezy's dancers?'

'Could be. But I recruited them because of their experience as Navy Seals.'

20

CHARLOTTE'S OFFER OVER BREAKFAST – SATURDAY 7:00AM

'Another coffee Charlotte?' Teal asked.

'Yes please. I've got a lot to do today.'

'More than yesterday?'

'Well, not more, but more *politically sensitive*. I need to call my parents and have a well thought through alternate story as to how I've spent these last four days.'

'Another string to your bow. Tell me Charlotte, what do you plan to do when you finish university?'

'Not one hundred percent sure yet but I'm thinking along the lines of a fashion design and fabric importing business.'

'Sounds wonderful. I could arrange start-up investment for you.'

'Wow. That would be...' Charlotte hesitated, 'in exchange for what?'

'Occasional information collection.'

'For which organisation?'

'I work for the Australian Department of Foreign Affairs and from time to time, the Australian Security Intelligence Organisation.'

'So, you're a spy?'

'We don't use that term. I'm an intelligence officer and, from time to time I'm asked to develop relationships and collect information on matters of national and international concern.'

'Again. Wow. You did seem a little out of place at that party in Rome.'

'Whereas you did not. As a model and fashion designer you would have access to a vast international industry.'

'This is not how I imagined my future.'

'Bien sûr que non. Of course not. Nor did you imagine that you would be rescuing more than a dozen girls from a life of slavery and rape.' Charlotte was taken back by the severity of this remark.

'What type of projects?'

'Projects where your role in the textile and fashion industry will mean that your presence is unremarkable.'

'Look. I'm flattered, but you don't know my family situation.'

'Of course I know your family situation. In fact, I know more about you and your parents than you know yourself.'

Charlotte shook her head. 'That doesn't surprise me. Even Maurice Morenzo knows more than I do.'

'Did you know that as a result of your efforts, he's been contained.'

'YES!' Charlotte cried out, throwing her pumped fists into the air.

'If you join us, you'll get the opportunity for more wins like this. Think about it. You don't need to make the decision today.' Teal looked at Charlotte thoughtfully. 'You know, you could do anything you wanted to. You're bright, inventive and courageous. Think about the legacy you wish to create.'

'You're clearly a master negotiator.'

'Maybe. Time will tell.' Teal smiled and looked at her watch. 'I need to go. I've got flights to arrange and a flotilla to meet. Jacques Dessault will be receiving quite the welcome this morning. See you shortly at the port of Messina.'

And then she was gone. Charlotte glanced at the local newspaper as she finished her breakfast. Her Italian was limited, but she was fairly sure that the heading of 'Terminato lo sciopero dei controllori del traffico aereo' was announcing that the air traffic controller strike was over.

21

SCOTT NEGOTIATES ON THE SAUDI
YACHT – FRIDAY 11:30PM

It hadn't been difficult to locate the yacht owned by the Saudi businessman. Working out their approach to getting an invite aboard had been more challenging.

'Ahoy there. We've come to collect some packages for Mr Morenzo,'

'Where's Luigi?'

'At the vineyard. There's been a security breach that needs attention.'

'Yes. I know about that. This is rather a late hour to call without advance notice.'

'Our apologies. Everything is happening in a rush.'

'OK. Send your dinghy over and I'll have the two girls ready.'

'Actually, we'd like to discuss the buy-back of the other two girls as well.'

'I see. Well, I need to let you know that I'm very happy with my purchases, but for the right price I could be persuaded to sell them back. You'd better come aboard.'

· · ·

Scott and Roy climbed aboard the dinghy and crossed the short distance between the two yachts.

'Wa alaykum a salaam. Hello and welcome aboard.' Scott and Roy removed their shoes and were greeted with very firm and long handshakes.

'Mr Morenzo has a lovely yacht,' said their host.

'Yes, he does. But I can see that your vessel also has superior lines and has been furnished with outstanding taste.' Roy bit the side of his cheek to stop himself from laughing at Scott's flattery, particularly because of the Arab's ostentatious taste.

'Do you have time to eat with us?'

'Of course, please allow us to wash our hands first.'

Their Saudi hosts, who'd introduced themselves as Saad and Ibrahim, smiled and showed them to the bathroom. Scott and Roy made a show of lathering up their hands to their elbows, and reviewed the yacht's layout carefully as they returned to the upper deck where they were invited to sit cross-legged around a low table. Falafels, martabuq and shawarma were presented on several beautiful plates.

'Can I offer you Arabic coffee or perhaps champagne?' Roy gave Scott a bewildered look. 'It's of course Saudi champagne, comprising apple juice, oranges, mint sprigs and lemonade, so it's non-alcoholic,' Saad explained.

'Thank you for your thoughtfulness Saad. Yes please for the champagne.' The champagne was served by a clearly nervous young woman wearing a gold embroidered kaftan style dress and hijab.

'And this is?'

'Layla,'

'And she is your...?'

'First purchase. I'm happy with her, and as I mentioned, would be reluctant to let her go.'

'And the other girls, would you kindly introduce us before we commence negotiations?'

'Of course.' He turned to Ibrahim and waved his hand. He left and returned moments later with another young woman.

'This is Fatimah.' The woman rolled her eyes.'

'Fiona is my name,' she said defiantly.

'And based on that accent, I'd say you were brought up in Ireland.'

'That would be true.'

'You know who you look like Fatimah, I mean Fiona?'

'Couldn't care less.'

'Saoirse Ronan, the American/Irish actor and star of *Little Women* and *The Way Back*. Have you seen her in either of these films?'

'I might have.'

'And don't you agree you look a lot like her, particularly in the second film?'

'Maybe,' she replied quietly, trying to guess why this man she didn't know was talking about films featuring independent women and a great escape.

'She's a handful this one,' said Saad, 'and while it would cause me great pain to let her go, I could accept it for the right compensation.'

'I see. I'm ready to begin negotiations. But first, a request. We only have a small dinghy so can I ask that Roy take the other two girls back to Mr Morenzo's yacht while we share expectations about the price of these assets?'

Saad hesitated. He preferred to keep all the girls together until the new deal was done and funds had been transferred.

'You know that he's not a patient man, Saad, which is why we've been sent to see you while Luigi sorts out the security problems. He wants all deals finalised as soon as possible so he can return to Corsica.'

'Very well. Ibrahim, can you get the packages and deliver them to the dinghy.' This language of *packages* irritated Scott immensely.

'So, it's my understanding you paid,' Scott hesitated, '$250,000 for Layla.'

'That is not true. I paid $300,000 for Layla, and Fatimah was thrown in as a thank you for collection services.'

'That's not what I was told. May I see your contract, please?' Saad left the room and could be heard riffling through papers. Scott glanced across the water and was pleased to see that Roy had the girls on the yacht. Saad returned and passed him the contract.

'Yes, you're right. Please accept my apologies. I feel it would be reasonable to offer you $300,000 for Layla and $100,000 for Fatimah.'

'This price does not adequately compensate me for either inconvenience or the great disappointment I feel at losing two such beautiful women, that I could surely sell for a higher price in my own country.'

'I'm sorry, Saad. But this is the highest rate I have approval for.' Scott shook his head and lowered his eyes.

'Sixt hundred thousand for both is the minimum I can part with them for.'

'I will need to speak with Mr Morenzo. Will you excuse me for a few minutes?'

'Of course. Take your time.' Scott walked out onto the deck and pulled his phone out. He kept talking until he could see that Roy had returned.

'All good?' Roy nodded.

'And how many staff are there below?'

'Three. A chef, waiter and the captain.'

'OK. Ready to give this a go?'

'Nope.'

'That's the spirit.' Scott walked back to join Saad on the upper deck.

'He has agreed to six hundred thousand, if you throw in this yacht.'

'What? That is outrageous!'

'Sir,' a deckhand interrupted their conversation. 'Another dinghy is approaching. Shall I allow them to board?'

'Who is it?'

'Luigi Rizzo.'

'Yes. Immediately. He will certainly convince Mr Morenzo to make a more acceptable offer.'

A horn sounded followed by screaming. The two girls on Scott's yacht had 'escaped' their bindings, started the engine and were now ramming the dinghy transporting Luigi and Marco.

'What the...? Roy, you idiot. You were meant to have secured the girls.' Scott raced to the rail to look at the spectacle, as did Saad, Ibrahim and the three other crew members. 'Turn to your left Luigi. Turn, turn...' Startled, Luigi looked at the man he did not know who was issuing instructions. At that moment, the girls were successful in tipping the dinghy. Luigi and Marco called out in anger as they hit the chilly water.

'Roy, go collect them. I don't think they can swim,' Roy rushed to the dinghy, grabbing Fatimah and Layla on his way.

'Sir,' the deckhand cried. 'The other two girls. They've been taken.' Saad pivoted in anger towards Scott who had already slipped away and dived off the bow of the yacht. He was nowhere to be seen in the dark water. Saad grabbed his gun and began shooting indiscriminately into the water.

'Don't shoot, don't shoot, Saad, it's us,' Luigi cried out. Saad looked at the men struggling in the water. He was furious and devoid of sympathy for their situation.

'We have to go before the coast guard arrives, Ibrahim. Leave them.'

Roy had a towel ready for Scott as he climbed out of the water. Saad's vessel was already moving away from their location at speed.

'They're going to have a few choice words for Mr Morenzo.'

'I wonder where he is?'

22

ARRIVING AT MESSINA PORT –
SATURDAY 8:00AM

'Over here,' came a familiar voice. Charlotte was not surprised to see Mason standing beside a cameraman on the port at Messina. 'We heard on the grapevine that Jack is back. Hoping you'd both be open to an exclusive interview.'

'You'll need to ask Jacques. My future career path requires a lower media profile,'

'What? No! And what direction is that?'

'Haven't decided, but definitely requiring a quieter social media presence.'

'But I've got a camera crew,' he pleaded. Charlotte looked at Mason for a moment before responding.

'I'll get you an interesting story. Give me a moment.' Charlotte called Channing, who was still at the hotel, but was as Charlotte expected, over the moon at the opportunity to chat with Mason and increase her influencer presence.

Teal was also at the port. Standing discreetly to the side with a few other people who were dressed for maximum anonymity. Quite a contrast to the way many Italians wore their finest clothes when out and about in town. Charlotte nodded and wondered what Teal was planning.

A long white boat with the words *Guardia Costeria* written in red on the side secured its moorings and two familiar faces disembarked. Charlotte wondered where the coast guard had picked up Luigi and Marco who were clearly not happy, clinging to grey blankets wrapped round their shoulders. As they approached, Luigi glanced towards her with cold eyes and shouted,

'Tu traditrice, you traitor!' Charlotte looked at Teal who was watching the exchange carefully. Charlotte lifted her index finger which was immediately understood as a cry for help. Two of the anonymous men standing beside Teal were quick to accompany the Monk's lieutenants off the pier.

'What just happened?' Mason asked.

'What d'ya mean?'

'Those men? The guys with the blankets.'

'Yeah?'

'They knew you. And not in a good way.'

'I don't know, but look, isn't that the yacht Scott was working on?' Mason swung around in anticipation to see a familiar yacht sliding into port.

'Yes,' he shouted gleefully. The yacht berthed and the first person off the boat was a shoeless Roy, followed by four young women who were bouncing from one foot to the other and laughing. When they saw Charlotte they shrieked and rushed over to hug her, nearly causing her to stumble.

'What's this?' Mason asked.

'Just a few friends I made in the modelling industry.' Charlotte hugged each one and directed them to Teal.

'OK. What's the story, Charlotte?' Mason said as he watched the girls giving their names to the elegantly dressed woman with the clipboard.

'Why don't you ask Scott and Roy?'

'Hey matey,' Mason called out to Scott as he walked across the pier and thumped him on the back. 'What've you been up to?'

'Ahh you know, going to rock concerts, dancing with beautiful girls, picking up stranded passengers.'

'And…?' Mason asked. 'I know there's more to this story.' Charlotte looked at Scott, raising her eyebrows ever so slightly and silently willing him not to reply.

'And Channing is just the person to ask. Here she comes.' Charlotte interrupted waving at her Ukrainian friend. 'Channing. Mason wants to interview you about your experience at the vineyard.'

'Of course,' she replied as though this is what she did every day. Scott, Roy and Charlotte watched Mason smoothly slip into interviewer mode.

'Roy.'

'Yes, Charlotte?'

'I'm pretty sure Niamh is on that yacht just about to berth over there.' Roy took off like a rabbit seeing a blade of grass poking through snow. Charlotte took a deep breath and smiled as she rested her hands on her head.

'You OK?' Scott asked.

'Of course. Why wouldn't I be?'

'My word. The situations you get yourself into. And out of. If only your parents knew.'

'Which of course they won't for reasons we both appreciate.'

He looked at her fondly. 'Mum's the word.' There was a long silence with each aware of how close they were standing to the other. Charlotte looked at the buttons on his shirt and continued talking, more nervously this time.

'Not too much trouble collecting the four girls from the Saudi sheik?'

'Nope, not too much resistance, although I had to get wet.'

'We watched a rather damp Luigi and Marco arrive about twenty minutes ago. They managed to get a lift with the coast guard. You all went swimming together?'

'I'll tell you over dinner. What are your plans now?'

Charlotte thought about saying she wanted to snuggle in close to those buttons. Before she could respond a gentleman standing behind them coughed.

'Excusez-moi. Sorry to disturb you. Mademoiselle Wyatt?'

'Oui. C'est moi.'

'My name is Victor Dessault. My wife and I would like to introduce ourselves and thank you. Jacques called and told us what you did, and well, it is hard to find the words. His yacht will arrive shortly and we were wondering if you would be free to join us for coffee, once he does?'

'Bien sûr. Of course.'

Scott and Charlotte watched Monsieur Dessault return to his wife a short distance away. She waved and blew Charlotte air kisses.'

'Now I need to speak to you immediately,' Scott said.

'Really. What do you want to tell me, Scott?' He stepped a little closer and hooked his finger through her belt. She looked at his stubbly chin and resisted the urge to touch it.

'I may have lied to your mother in order to get her and your Dad out of Brisbane.'

'Uh-huh. And ...'

'I may have said that we were getting closer and that we

were planning on making an announcement to both sets of parents, together, at Evans Head this coming Thursday.'

'What sort of announcement?'

'Well, that's something I need to discuss with you.' Charlotte's heart skipped a beat. She stood very still and looked at him unblinking. 'I can't come back to Australia now. I need to get this yacht ready to sail to Palermo, and after that we're headed for Greece. I still have one thousand kilometres to sail, and exams to sit before I can get my captain's licence. You know that's my focus, for now. And then I'll be able to take a break. I know Miranda's planning a holiday in Thailand. And I know that she's hoping that you, Mason, and I will be free to come. I want to. It'd be nice to spend time together when we're not... when we're not distracted.'

'Hmmm.' Charlotte purred as she leant in against his chest. 'Yes. That would be nice. And what do you propose I tell our parents this Thursday?'

'You have a remarkable talent for extracting yourself from difficult situations. I know you'll think of something.' His hand moved from her belt to her waist and he leant in and put his lips softly on hers, leaving them there for a moment, before kissing her on the cheek.

'Jacques is back,' Ayeesha shouted. Charlotte's head was spinning. She turned to see Ayeesha standing with Roy and Jacques' parents a short distance away. Niamh was first off the boat, rushing into her brother's arms. Roy was whooping with joy and passed his sister his mobile phone so she could call their parents. Jacques walked slowly down the gang plank, looking for someone. Teal waved and Jacques pointed back into the yacht with his thumb, before providing the universal *thumbs up* sign. As Jacques disembarked, he kissed his parents and then looked over at Charlotte. He asked to be excused for a moment and ran towards her and swung her round and round like a swing at a carnival.

'You are so wonderful,' he whispered, 'I'm so lucky I found that bottle.' Mason was ecstatic as the camera rolled, particularly as he was the only journalist on the port.

'Enough, enough! Put me down, Jacques,' Charlotte cried out, laughing. A small crowd gathered, clapping and thinking this a most wonderful romantic gesture.

'Now let's get a couple more photos,' Mason directed. 'Who else needs to be included?' Jacques immediately signalled to Ayeesha and Niamh to join them. They placed their arms around each other, and couldn't help but smile. 'And how should I label this photo?'

'Charlie and her angels,' Jacques announced loudly.

'So, does that make you Bosley, from the TV series?'

'No. I'm Jack and I'm of no consequence. Shine the light on these wonderous ladies.'

'And on these,' Charlotte said, waving at Channing, Rowan, Paisley and Mackenzie and inviting them to gather for a photo. 'They're the winners of the Escape from the Vineyard Challenge.'

'Not heard of that one,' Mason said.

'I'll brief you later,' Charlotte replied while watching Mr Morenzo being removed from the yacht in handcuffs by Teal's associates, followed shortly afterwards by Rex, the captain and waiter. The chef was carried out on a stretcher. With all the girls laughing and taking photos, Charlotte momentarily lost sight of Scott. She stepped aside from the crowd and spotted him shaking hands with Roy. Scott was about to leave. He looked slightly towards her, waved, and then walked back onto his yacht.

What the heck? Charlotte thought, walking over to the edge of the port to watch him prepare to leave. She put her hands up in the air, questioningly and then pulled out her phone and texted him.

You promised me dinner?

No reply.

'That's the juicy guy you danced with at the Breezy concert isn't it?' Rowan asked.

'Yep,' Charlotte replied.

'And what's the nature of your relationship?'

'I have no idea. Any other questions?' Charlotte replied more tersely than she intended.

'Well yes. We were wondering what our prize was for winning the competition.'

'Just got a few final details to sort out and I'll be announcing the prize to everyone at the hotel at 11:00am. Can you make sure that Mackenzie, Paisley and Channing are there?'

'You bet.' Rowan raced back to tell her friends the good news as Charlotte's phone rang.

'Hi Mum. How's things?'

'Super. We're having such a nice time here at Evans Head. I have three bream in the basket waiting to be cooked for dinner. It's so lovely here. Scott's parents are enjoying the break as well.'

'And Miranda?'

'She's arriving tomorrow.'

'That's great. Did you hear the news?' Charlotte asked.

'And what news might that be?' her mother asked tentatively.

'That the air traffic strike is resolved and I can come home now.'

'Yes. We'd heard that. About time. Anything else?' Melissa Wyatt asked softly. Charlotte hesitated.

'It'll probably take me a day to two to get on the plane

because of the number of flights that have been cancelled. I also need to arrange transfer from Messina to Rome.'

'What have you been doing in Sicily?' Charlotte knew that her mother was *fishing* so gave her an answer she would appreciate.

'Spending time with Scott.' Her mother gently tutted, signalling approval.

'Gotta go pack now Mum. Love to Dad. See you Thursday. Bye.'

'Safe travels, honey.'

23

BACK ON THE TAORMINA TRIUMPH –
SATURDAY 9:00AM

Charlotte let Mason take two photos with the Dessault family before she scooted him off the yacht with instructions to meet her at the hotel at 11:00 am for an exciting announcement. He pushed her for more details but she remained tight-lipped, which was easy because she'd not yet worked out what message she'd be delivering. With Mason gone, she turned her focus to Jacques' family, who were treating her like royalty. They had arranged delivery of a champagne morning tea to the *Taormina Triumph*. They wanted to know everything about her, including the circumstances under which she'd met Jacques and of her plans for the future. Charlotte provided an abridged version of her family's history, spending more time describing her confusion at which subjects to study and her interest in fashion design.

'What an extraordinary story from a truly remarkable young woman. I'm certain that you can achieve anything you set your mind to – and we'd like to help.' He pushed a white envelope across the table and watched with delight as she opened it. Charlotte nearly fell off her chair when she saw the number on the cheque inside.

'No, no, no, this is too much.' She put the cheque back in the envelope and passed it back. 'However, I'm in a bit of a difficult situation and if you would be open to an *in kind* gift, that would help me.'

'Of course. What do you have in mind?' Charlotte explained her need for prizes.

'Your request is very modest. Further,' he said reaching into his pocket, 'if at any point in the future you are in need of additional resources to get you out of a tricky situation, I want you to ask us. Any time of the day or night. Here are my details,' he said handing her his business card.

'Yes, Monsieur Dessault. Thank you.'

There were long hugs as she said goodbye to Jacques and his parents. Niamh and Roy were waiting to board as she left the yacht and they kissed each other on both cheeks as they said goodbye.

'Keep out of trouble now. No more accepting rides on yachts,' Roy said with a playful wag of his finger.

As she walked up the port, she wasn't surprised to see Mason waiting for her.

'Thought we could share a taxi back to your hotel and that maybe you could give me a few hints about what you plan to announce.'

Charlotte punched him playfully in the arm. 'Do you ever give up?'

'I could ask the same about you, Miss Wyatt.'

There was a small crowd waiting excitedly in the Europa Palace Hotel lobby. Some of the rescued girls were already on flights back home, having completed interviews with Interpol.

'Thank you to those who participated both knowingly and unknowingly in the vineyard escape game. I know it was very difficult and stressful for many of you and I want to congratulate you on your resilience, creativity and team-work.' A round of applause followed. 'It has been deter-mined that four prizes are to be awarded. These are for Channing, Mackenzie, Paisley and Rowan. You have each been given the use of the *Taormina Triumph* yacht for you and up to ten of your friends, for a one-week cruise anywhere in Europe. The prize includes all flight transfers, food and drinks while you're on board.' There were gasps followed by a stunned silence and then shrieking as the girls jump up and down. Mason caught the joy on his phone. 'And this gift has been generously provided by the Dessault family.' Whoops of laughter accompanied a more enthusi-astic round of applause. As the crowd started to disperse Charlotte walked over to Ayeesha. 'Monsieur Dessault would also like to provide you with financial assistance to complete your law studies, by way of thank you.' Ayeesha embraced her friend.

'I'll never forget you,' Ayeesah said.

'Let's keep in touch. Who knows, we may be able to help each other out again in the future. Have you seen Niamh?'

'She's probably with Jacques.' Ayeesha replied.

'Jacques?'

'Yep. They got kinda close when we were imprisoned together. Suspect she'll be having her own private cruise with Mr Dessault junior in the not-too-distant future, once she's spent some time back home with her folks.'

'Oh. I love a happy ending.'

'And you Charlotte? What sort of ending will you be celebrating after this four-day fiasco?'

'Getting on that plane. Getting home. Spending time with Mum and Dad.'

'Anything else?'

'Perhaps. We'll see.' Charlotte's phone pinged interrupting their conversation. She looked at the message and smiled.

Reservation for 2 by the water
Baitoey Seafood Restaurant. Krabi.
7:00pm. 20 January

24

AT ROME AIRPORT

Not surprisingly, Rome airport was busy. It was hard to believe that only six days had passed since she was last here. As she'd done on her last visit, she picked up several magazines and newspapers for the flight home. Channing was grinning from ear to ear on the cover of *Hello*. She'd achieved her nirvana. She was now a major celebrity on social media for her role in helping the girls to break out of the vineyard's basement. Mason had written quite a piece and was proud to report that she was to be the host of a reality TV show called *Roman Roulette*, where participants had to escape from a *difficult situation*. It wasn't an original idea but a popular one. Mason called as she finished reading his article.

'Hello there. Congratulations on your piece. Looks good. What did your boss say?'

'She was chuffed. Still waiting to see end of week sales figures of course, but very pleased with early sales. Hey. Did you know that Channing is going to use her one week cruising prize to host a media extravaganza, and that yours truly has already been invited? Best junket ever. Can't wait.'

'It's not going to interfere with the trip Miranda is planning to Thailand is it?'

'Nah. Cruise is in July, while our south-east Asian adventure is during the cool season.'

'Looking forward to it. As is Miranda.'

'And Scott too,' Mason added. Charlotte asked if he knew what the three Scottish girls were planning for their prize cruise.

'I understand they're going to combine the three weeks and take their families around the Mediterranean.'

'Lovely. Family is so important.'

'Excited to get home to Oz?' Mason asked.

'That's an understatement.'

'Sorry. I've got another call on the line Charlotte. Gotta go. See you in Krabi in January.'

'You bet.' Charlotte put the phone in her bag and clicked through the other magazines. There was an article about Ayeesha in *The Economist*. She had been delighted to have been part of an operation that hurt the slavery trade. She had highlighted the need for more countries to do more to combat this awful business with a need for more resources dedicated to eliminating slavery worldwide.

'You know, you could continue to disrupt the slavery trade.' Charlotte looked up at the other traveller. She was no longer surprised to meet Teal Dubios when she least expected it. 'Have you thought more about my offer?'

'A little, but I've made no decision either way.'

'Charlotte Wyatt. You're a woman of many talents. You achieved something remarkable, without violence. We were so inspired by the way you encouraged the girls to fight back. We'd our eye on the operation for a while and had wanted to bring the entire network down, rather than picking off a few criminals. You were such a valuable asset, as was Breezy. We reached out to her when we heard she'd performed at the vineyard. When she heard about the trafficking, she welcomed the opportunity to be involved. This was her first and maybe her last project. We'll see. Can I ask you a question?'

'Of course.'

'Are you in a relationship?'

Charlotte thought about Scott.

'No. I'm not in a relationship.'

'Keep it that way for now. It's easier.'

25

EVANS HEAD

'She's here,' Melissa Wyatt called out to her husband from the veranda of their cabin at Evans Head. She jumped over the three steps onto the path and embraced her daughter.

'Not so tight Mum. Can't breathe.'

'Oy. My turn now. Move aside woman,' Charlotte's father said, walking down the steps. Her mother released her and she embraced her father in a side-wobble hug.

'What's this?' he asked flicking her short hair. 'Each time you come back from Europe you've changed.'

'What can I say, Dad? One needs to try new things.'

'I like it. Very Audrey Hepburn in the movie ...' he hesitated.

'*Roman Holiday*. I know. We both experienced a change of life in Italy. What about life here? How's the fishing?' she asked.

'Fantastic. They've been hopping on the line. But don't go changing the topic on me. How was Sicily and what did you do? You must have been busy, we barely heard from you. Not even a text.'

'Sorry about that. It was a bit full on, what with visits to vineyards, dancing at rock concerts and making new friends.'

'And Scott was there?'

'You know he was there, Dad. As was Mason. Where's Miranda?' Charlotte asked changing the conversation.

'With her parents at the surf. They were hoping you'd bring Scott home.'

'He's still focussed on getting his captain's qualifications for the moment.'

'Does he have long to go?' her mother asked.

'Couple of months I would think. Depends on how many trips he does.'

'Oh,' said Melissa, not sure what to say next.

'I'm pretty sure he's going to join our call tonight Mum. He always enjoys speaking with you. 'Look. Here comes Miranda. I'll check with her.'

'Welcome home world traveller,' Miranda called out to her friend. What news do you bring me of exciting adventures, exotic places and interesting men?'

'Well Mason is fine, which I know is really the question you wanted answered. He's as charming and persistent as ever. I think his role of investigative journalist suits him. Still single I believe and interested in the holiday you're planning for the four of us in the Kingdom of Thailand.'

'Did he mention me?'

'Yes, when we spoke about the holiday. Like your brother, I think his primary focus is on his career for now.'

'Ah. So, you two didn't...'

'We danced, together and around each other. I don't know. Like both of them I'm more focussed on my career for the moment.'

'Have you made any decisions career-wise while you were away?'

'Partly. I'll share my thoughts tonight.'

'Everyone's very much looking forward to the announcement.'

Charlotte inwardly groaned.

'Hi Bro,' Miranda said smiling at her brother's image on Facetime. 'Where are you?'

'In Palermo, shortly to depart for Catania.'

'Charlotte says that you had a great time in Taormina.'

'Did she? What else did she say?'

'You can ask her yourself.' Miranda thrust the tablet in Charlotte's face.

'Hi.'

'Hello there.'

'Good trip home?'

'Uneventful. Just the way I like it.'

'I doubt that.'

Charlotte sucked her bottom lip and smiled. 'You ready to share the good news with our folks?'

'Of course. Attention everyone. You're probably wondering why we summoned you all to Evans Head. Well, while she's been away, Charlotte has made a decision about the direction of her life.' Their parents swapped excited glances. 'As you know, Charlotte started studying fashion, then swapped to digital media, then examined a hybrid option. The trip overseas has made her realize that fashion is her passion. And I'm delighted to report that we are going to become partners. In fact, I'll be the first investor in her new design business that will from this day forward, be known as *Chic Charlie*. Please join with me in raising your glass to her success.' Their parents were a little bewildered. 'To Chic Charlie,' Scott repeated.

'Hear hear, chin chin,' Miranda responded, lifting up her cup of tea.

'You two are certainly full of surprises,' Andrew Wyatt remarked while ruffling his daughter's hair and looking at his wife. Melissa Wyatt shrugged her shoulders.

'Wonderful to have you safely home, love.'

'Couldn't agree more, Mum.'

EPILOGUE

K rabi, Thailand – nine months later

Scott's kiss goodbye at Krabi airport had made Charlotte weak at the knees. It was a fitting end to a wonderful week of snorkelling and snuggling up around a fire on the beach. Many events looked forward to in life failed to meet expectations, but not this time. She and Scott had spent the week talking, and other things. She was still thinking about the *other things* when her phone rang, breaking her reverie-like state.

'How are you enjoying Thailand, Charlotte?' asked Teal. Charlotte was not in the least surprised that Teal Dubois knew where she was.

'It's been wonderful.'

'Do you mind staying in Southeast Asia a little longer? I've a job for you. Someone important is missing in Myanmar.

SONG REFERENCE

'Over Byron Bay: I didn't know I loved you' words and score by Jane Ellyson. Recorded by Rob Snarski. Listen on Bandcamp.

https://janeellyson.bandcamp.com/releases

Five years have slowly past
Since you went away,
Although I feel your presence
At the strangest times each day.
It's like you whisper in my ear
When I think of anything insincere,
Or I sing along to a favourite song
And then I remember that you're gone.

I didn't know I loved you
Until you went away.
With a hole in my life, I've come to regret
The things I didn't say.

I think of you and wonder if you ever think of me
It's too late now
We've missed our time
As you're no longer free.
Will I ever get a second chance
To tell you how I feel?
Cause what I mistook for friendship
Was a deeper love, so real.

I didn't know I loved you
Until you went away.
With a hole in my life, I've come to regret
The things I didn't say.

I'm thinking of you now
On this gorgeous, deep blue day,
Breathing in the northern beauty
Looking out over Byron Bay.

I didn't know I loved you
Until you went away.
With a hole in my life, I've come to regret
The things I didn't say.
The things I didn't say
… didn't say

THANKS FOR READING

I hope you enjoyed reading *Roman Roulette* as much as I did writing it. I'd love to know what you thought of the story if you have the time to pen me a few lines. I get a kick out of chatting with readers.

Email me at janeellyson@gmail.com

If you enjoyed the story, please tell your friends and write a review online. You can do this on Goodreads (link above) or wherever you bought the book.

The sequels to *Roman Roulette* include *Missing in Myanmar* and *Nonsense in the North*.

Happy reading,
Best Jane
www.janeellyson.com

ABOUT JANE ELLYSON

Jane has a deep connection to the Far North Coast of New South Wales where several of her novels are set. Her great grandparents owned a farm a little way out of Byron Bay and her grandparents were long term residents of Mullumbimby. She currently lives at Possum Creek, not far out of Bangalow – well she would if she was real – rather than being the pen name of someone who would prefer to remain anonymous. This is her third novel.

Boy from Bangalow (Prequel)

Melissa Bourne meets her neighbour Andrew Wyatt during orientation week at university. He's cute confident and her adversary in the Great Debate. Will the right sparks fly?

Over Byron Bay (Book 1 of 5)

Melissa Bourne and Andrew Wyatt were neighbours in the country town of Bangalow in Australia. Friends, good friends were all they'd ever been. This situation suited them both until Andrew found someone else. Surprised at her jealousy and with an international job offer in hand, Melissa left the country. She accepted a job offer in Boston, met Jonathan Brinkley, married and settled into life in the U.S.

Five years later she returns to Bangalow for a visit with her father, shortly after the death of Andrew's mother. The two meet briefly at the funeral, and the day before she flies back to Boston providing an opportunity to rekindle their relationship and to recognise that their feelings for each other go beyond friendship. Melissa returns to the States in turmoil.

Substitute Child (Book 2 of 5)

A deckhand in France discovers a bottle with a letter inside. The bottle has floated all the way from Byron Bay in Australia to the south of France. The discovery prompts a whirlwind journey for Charlotte Wyatt into the world of paparazzi, European royalty and the criminal underworld.

Substitute Child is the story of a student travelling to the other side of the world to collect a bottle with a love letter to a brother she never knew and a journey to discover who she is and what she wants from her life.

Missing in Myanmar (Book 4 of 5)

Charlotte Wyatt wasn't sure what she was letting herself in for when she agreed to be available for occasional information gathering activities for the Australian Securities Intelligence Organisation. Her first assignment comes at the end of a holiday in Thailand. Having just said goodbye to her boyfriend, who has taken a job sailing from Port Vila in Vanuatu to Bundaberg in Australia, Charlotte Wyatt is intrigued by the opportunity to go to Myanmar to gather information about a missing person.

With the help of a mysterious librarian, she finds the information she was sent to retrieve, and then, just as she's making plans to return, the lights go out in Myanmar and the military takes over. With a reluctant passenger, Charlotte runs checkpoints and dodges bullets, in a race to the border.

Nonsense in the North (Book 5 of 5)

The Australian bush has a reputation for being dangerous what with snakes, spiders and stinging trees – and that's just the start of it.

A too-good-to-be-true sailing trip results in Scott's disappearance from waters near Hamilton Island in Australia. Now considered by police to be an integral part of an international drug smuggling operation, Charlotte relies on a sympathetic police officer and an aboriginal tracker named 'Nonsense' to travel deep into Cape Conway, to disrupt a drug exchange and to find her Scott, improving their chances of a happily-ever-after. All the while helping plan her best friend's wedding.

~

www.janeellyson.com

www.ingramcontent.com/pod-product-compliance
Lightning Source LLC
Chambersburg PA
CBHW020642130726
47903CB00003BA/949